HOW TO

A TAX-EFFICI... WILL

HOW TO WRITE
A TAX-EFFICIENT WILL

Deborah Bowers

(2nd Edition)

DEDICATION

To everyday families.

TABLE OF CONTENTS

DISCLAIMER

This book is intended as a general guide, not legal, inheritance tax, or other professional advice. The complexity of the principles herein has been watered down in the interest of clarity while maintaining the core principles.

This publication does not provide a complete view of all areas of Will writing or inheritance tax, nor are those areas of the law addressed in every detail. Inheritance tax is an ever-changing dimension of law. The law of Wills may change with time, but every effort has been made while writing to represent the current state of the law.

The names used in this book are fictitious and are not personally known to me, nor do they refer to anyone in society. Persons reading this work should not assume that the examples given are connected to them in any way.

The examples are randomly chosen for illustrative purposes only.

This guide is intended to discuss matters of Will writing and inheritance tax applicable to England and Wales. Reference may be made to the law of Scotland, where the considerations governing the writing of Wills and the law of intestacy differ to some degree from the laws of England and Wales. Where reference is made to Scottish Wills, the applicable practices in Scotland will be discussed.

Readers are advised to seek independent professional advice or verify this book's content before relying on its content. The Author has made every effort to ensure that the information contained in this book is applicable and accurate as of the date of publication; however, the Author will be exempt from liability in relation to any reliance placed on the contents of this book which results in economic or other loss.

The validity of a Will depends on it complying with the law, case law, or judicial precedents. The law and guidance are subject to change as parliament reviews and amends legislation. Readers are reminded to ensure they comply with acceptable standards and principles of validity at all times. Every effort has been made to reflect current laws and best practices in this work.

In publishing this book, the Author has relied upon her experience in the field of Will Writing, her knowledge, having successfully completed the Advanced Will Writing Exams of the Society of Trust and Estate Practitioners, frequently referred to as (STEP), and her training as a Solicitor of England and Wales. However, the Author acknowledges that based on the circumstances and needs of a client, the ability to write a tax-efficient Will can be a complex and intricate matter or as straightforward as ABC. Everyone's circumstances are different, and only after carefully considering the client's circumstances will a Will

Writer be in a position to provide specific advice instead of the general and generic advice provided herein.

INTRODUCTION

In 2020, with the arrival of coronavirus (COVID-19) in the United Kingdom, I began to receive increased calls from friends and relatives who wanted to understand how to write a Will and the impact of inheritance tax on their decisions. It occurred to me that I was not aware of any book that brings these two things together in a manner that everyday families can understand, appreciate, and apply.

Many books on Will writing are generally too taxing for most to read, and to get real value, you may need to part with a bit more cash than you can afford in these challenging times. This is because many such texts cater to the Will Writing Practitioner, not the everyday family.

The field of inheritance tax is complex and is subject to change with each budget, thus adding to the confusion and intimidation for most families when they begin to think about writing a tax-efficient Will. I, therefore, decided to embark upon writing this book in an attempt to bridge this gap.

Families are reminded to seek independent legal advice. This book offers clarity concerning the matters to be considered and the steps to be taken to ensure that your Will reflects your wishes, having taken into account your inheritance tax position. This book arms readers with knowledge that may enable them to feel confident enough to undertake the writing of their own Will. Alternatively, it may put them in a position to speak confidently with a Will Writing Practitioner, posing relevant questions, thereby achieving their desired outcome.

It should be remembered that a Will takes effect at the death of the person who wrote it. Discussions of instruments such as Trust are discussed in this work in relation to how a trust is created in your will to take effect upon death. In this 2023/2024 second edition of "How to Write a Tax-Efficient Will," we discuss new matters such as "Lasting Powers of Attorney". We are all aging, and you may already have responsibility for an aging parent or grandparent. It is important that we understand how Lasting Powers of Attorney (LPA) can be used. They are not just essential for aging people; even young persons can put them in place as a security measure to protect their families. You will also be provided with references to get further information.

It is not possible to cover all eventualities. Still, every effort has been made to discuss the subject of Wills through the life of an everyday person, who may start as single, form a relationship, experience divorce or a breakup, or just live with another in a common law relationship.

The world is diverse, and we often think the grass is greener on the other side. This may persuade us to purchase a home abroad, where we can enjoy a bit of sun, sea, and sand. The impacts of such changes are not discussed in any detail here.

In such circumstances, it is best to consult the laws of the territory where the property has been purchased.

Further, we never really know who we may fall in love with. This book covers having a spouse or civil partner who is not British or not a UK domicile. The use of technical language has been avoided as much as possible, but some words such as "domicile" cannot be avoided. As you read this book, you may recall the dilemma of the wife of the former Chancellor of the Exchequer, Rishi Sunak, who was not obliged to pay tax in the United Kingdom as she was a foreign domicile. Knowledge of the rules surrounding domicile can be a great tax-saving tactic when you have a spouse from a foreign jurisdiction. The rules do not apply to every foreign jurisdiction, but would it not be good to know if it applies to your circumstances?

For more complex circumstances where there is a business to take into account or a provision to be made for a disabled child or children, it may be best to speak with your Tax Advisor, Will Writing Practitioner or Estate Planning Solicitor. Such matters will be addressed here only to the extent necessary to alert the reader to seek specialist advice or raise matters for consideration.

This book is written with the law of England and Wales in mind, but reference is made to the laws of Scotland and how it addresses some of the concerns raised herein, such as intestacy or dying without a will. The main difference is that a person aged sixteen can hold property in Scotland, whereas in England and Wales, the age of majority is eighteen years old. Additionally, the distribution of your estate on intestacy is different in Scotland compared to England and Wales.

A flowchart has been provided in the Appendix for both Scotland and England. Frequently forgotten are the rules relating to domicile when advising those from Scotland on the importance of drafting a Will. If they are found to be domiciled in Scotland at the time of death and have failed to write a Will, their estate will be distributed in accordance with the intestacy rules of Scotland, despite them possibly having lived in England and Wales for many years. This is valuable advice that must be explored or given to all Scots when considering the necessity for a Will. The Scots do not escape the 40% inheritance tax should their estates meet the relevant criteria.

You may subscribe and follow me on YouTube, where you will find valuable free content by searching for Deborah Bowers Channel.

Or by visiting:
https://www.youtube.com/channel/UCgJHrKI6u7CocwKS_3KUkVw
Or join my Facebook group: "Tax Efficient Wills UK"

Remember, anyone can write a valid Will if they follow the formalities, but not everyone can write a tax- efficient Will.

CHAPTER 1

WHY WRITE A WILL?

In this chapter, we shall discuss what a Will is, whether you should consider writing one, and how writing one may help you save on inheritance tax. We shall also look at what criteria need to be satisfied to ensure that your Will is valid.

This is not a book intended to instruct you on the law of Wills, but rather one aiming to bridge the gap in the minds of most people, between Will writing and inheritance tax. Discussions on the law will be brief, restricted to necessary guidance, to assist the reader's understanding of common terms used in Will writing.

A Will is a declaration of how you would like your assets to be managed or distributed on your death.

If you have not made a Will at the time of your death, your assets will be divided in accordance with the laws of intestacy, which apply to the jurisdiction where you are domiciled. For example, if you have lived in England and Wales all your life, then your property will be distributed per the laws governing the distribution of assets when a person dies without a Will in England and Wales. This is what is commonly refer to as "Intestate." For those who live in Scotland or are domiciled there, their assets will be determined following the laws of intestacy in Scotland.

In Appendix IV, I have provided a chart showing how the law of England and Wales distributes the assets of a person who has died without a Will in England and Wales. In Appendix V, there is a chart showing how the law of Scotland distributes the assets of a person who has died without a Will in Scotland.

There are a few critical things that one needs when deciding to write a Will. The first point we will discuss here is one's financial position. It is a good idea to have an appreciation of your net worth. Many people believe they are not worth much, own nothing, and do not need a Will. You may be surprised to realise that you are worth much more than you imagined.

Alternatively, you may be surprised to realise that you are worth much less. The beauty of writing a Will lies in the fact that you could be making provision for property that you may have received unexpectedly. In order to get an idea of what you are worth, you can complete the simple assets and liabilities sheet, which can be found at the back of this book in Appendix I.

The second thing to remember is the rules surrounding the validity of a Will in England and Wales. English law does not require special qualifications to enable someone to write a Will. Anyone can write their Will. The law, however, places great emphasis on whether or not a Will is valid. So, if you are concerned about writing a Will which does not render itself open to flimsy challenges, you should be certain to follow the formalities required to ensure the validity of your Will.

The important things to remember when writing a Will are that:

1. You should make or write your Will of your own volition. It should be your decision to write your Will.
2. You should be sane when you write your Will. You should not be suffering from any mental delusions.
3. You understand exactly what you are doing and the consequences of the distributions you are making in your Will.
4. You should comply with the right formalities for signing a Will in your jurisdiction, thereby ensuring its validity when you are no longer with us.

5. You should intend, by complying with the formalities for making a Will, to give effect to your Will.

In England and Wales, you need to ensure that when you sign your Will, you do so in the presence of two people present at the same time, who see you sign the Will and who sign as your witnesses in your presence during the same sitting. So, all three of you must be present together and see what each other is doing, knowing that you are doing so to give effect to the Will. This does not mean that your witnesses must know the contents of your Will.

Further, you should ensure that none of your witnesses are beneficiaries or stand to gain anything from your Will. In other words, the persons who witness you signing your Will should not be given a benefit or any gifts in your Will.

Ensure that the witnesses have nothing to gain from your Will.

There could be variations or exceptions to how a Will may be deemed valid, given various signing scenarios, but I would advise that you stick to the description given above to ensure validity in accordance with the laws of England and Wales.

The witnesses should also not be the husband, wife, or civil partner of any person you have gifted property in the Will. If this was the case, the Will might remain valid, but the gift to the witness's husband, wife, or partner could fail.

Use witnesses who are unlikely to benefit directly or indirectly from your Will.

It is also important that your witnesses fully appreciate what they are participating in; sighted witnesses are recommended, and persons who can read and write and who are not suffering from any mental disorders. It is imperative that your witnesses should be reliable and able to substantiate – by giving evidence in court as to how your Will was attested – should the need arise.

Thirdly, as far as English law is concerned, your property is yours, and you may do with it what you will, subject to a few adjustments a court could make based on a case-by-case basis, such as making provisions for dependents. However, before delving into our various examples of Wills, based on the life of "Jane," let us do some preparatory work, defining some commonly used terms in Will writing, some inheritance tax essentials, and the groundwork which may assist you before you embark upon writing your Will. It is good to understand the roles all persons mentioned in your will play.

In Appendix I, I have provided a checklist to be completed setting out your assets. This will help you arrive at your net worth. In Appendix II, I have provided a form to guide you on what you should consider before giving instructions to the Drafter. By completing these two forms, you will be ready with the information needed to get your will off to a great   start.

CHAPTER 2

ROLES PEOPLE PLAY

Everyone mentioned in your Will has a role to play. It is important that you gain an understanding of those roles as you may be drafting your own Will. Understanding who is doing what also demystifies the choppy waters of Will writing. Here I have described in simple terms the main roles and given some useful tips – or golden nuggets – to help you on your Will writing journey.

Testator/Testatrix

If you are a man writing a Will, you will be referred to as the Testator.

If you are a woman writing a Will, you will be referred to as the Testatrix.

The plural of Testator is Testators, and the plural of Testatrix is Testatrices. Still, these terms are used less frequently these days, and it is acceptable to use the word Testators when referring to male or female Will Maker.

Executor/Executrix

As the Will is intended to come into effect upon your death, it is important that you appoint persons to administer your estate or property after you are gone, in accordance with the intentions you have expressed in your Will. If you were to appoint one person to carry out this role, they would be referred to as the Executor if that person was a male and Executrix if that person was a female. If two or more persons are appointed to carry out that role, they are referred to in the plural as Executors.

The Executor is responsible for doing all the leg work of identifying and gathering your assets and liabilities, disposing of your corpse, organising the funeral, and ensuring that your Will is probated. This is an important role. If you intend to appoint two persons in this role, to act together, assure yourself beforehand that they will get along. Choose people who are accustomed to taking on responsibility. Avoid all procrastinators. You may, however, appoint a maximum of four Executors.

It is common to have your appointed Executors appointed as your Trustees. This means you will have fewer people involved in getting the work done. You can do this by simply stating that you would like to appoint as your Trustees those of your Executors who obtain probate of your Will, or you may appoint different persons entirely. In this book, the examples appoint the same persons as Trustees and Executors of the Will in all examples given.

Tip:

It is best to appoint two persons who will hold each other accountable where you have made several distributions or gifts in your Will to various persons.

Where, however, you want to give all of your estate or property to only one person who is an adult at the time you are either considering writing or writing the Will, it is best to simply appoint the one person whom you intend to give all as the Executor or Executrix.

Trustee/Trustees

The Trustee(s) is the person or persons who will become the Guardians of your property once the Executors have completed the leg work and obtained probate. They are responsible for ensuring that the property becomes vested into the names of those you left it for. They are called Trustees as the property is not theirs. They have only been entrusted with it to carry out your wishes. You can appoint a maximum of four Trustees.

Tip:

It is common practice to appoint your Executors as your Trustees. The same persons can perform both roles. Should you wish to appoint different persons, you are free to do so.

Beneficiary/Beneficiaries

The person to whom you have made a gift in your Will is called a Beneficiary. If you were to write:

"I give my house Chatswood Cottage, located at 150 Grove Road, to my son Richard Longwood."

Richard would be referred to as a Beneficiary in your Will. Where you have made gifts to several persons under the terms of your Will, they will collectively be referred to as Beneficiaries.

Guardian/Guardians

A Guardian is a person who will take on your parental responsibility towards your child should you pass while your child is still a minor. It is important to appoint Guardians if you have minor children at the time of writing your Will.

Remember that married parents have joint parental responsibility. In the case of single parents, where the other biological parent is not known or recorded on the birth certificate, the single parent will have parental responsibility. Where the child has lived with a single parent, but the other parent is known and recorded on the birth certificate, that other parent will need to be consulted as to whether they wish to take on parental responsibility. They may decline the responsibility but would have the right of first refusal unless they had been proven unfit or were currently unable to take on the role – due to being incarcerated, for example.

However, by appointing a Guardian, you are able to identify who you would like to give parental responsibility over your child or children. Choose someone loved by the children and who will treat them as their own. Remember that the initial funds to care for the children will come from your estate, but should your estate run out of funds, the Guardian will be left to bare the financial responsibility. You may appoint two people or more to be Guardians of the children, but you need to remember some very important things when appointing Guardians.

Tip:

The children will only be able to live in one location. So, if you were to appoint Tom Jones who lives at 86 Grove Road and Tracy Chapman who lives at 97 Watford Manor, to look after the child or children, a decision would need to be made as to where the child/children will live. It would be best to select the Guardians within a priority order. This means that you may select Tom Jones who lives at 86 Grove Road as the first Guardian, and should he be unwilling or unable to act, you would then select Tracy Chapman who lives at 97 Watford Manor, as Guardian.

Tip:

When choosing a couple to act as Guardians, you may name them both as joint Guardians of the child or children, as they live at the same address, but seriously consider which one of them you would like the children to live with in the unlikely event of a divorce. You can then name that person as Guardian, as the child or children will be placed to live with that person; it matters not if the other partner is also present. Marriages can be so unpredictable these days but do satisfy yourself that the current partner of the person you have appointed as Guardian would be happy to raise the child or children and welcome them into their home.

Tip:

People often wonder whether or not the Guardian will need to provide for the child or children you have left in their care. The straight answer is "YES" and "No." The money to provide for the child/children will come from your estate/property. For example, if the Guardian lives in a one-bed cottage and you have left five children to be cared for, with a twelve-bedroom house for the benefit of the children, then the Guardian may relocate to the home which you have left behind to live with the children and provide or supervise their care. The best interests of the children are what matters at all times.

Tip:

Ask your proposed Guardian whether or not he/she would be willing to undertake the responsibility before you make an appointment. Make no assumptions.

Tip:

If you plan to choose a Guardian older than you by a generation, be sure to choose a second option, should the first option predecease you or be unwilling or unable to act.

Tip:

Revocation of your Will automatically revokes any guardianship appointment which you have made under the terms of your Will unless a contrary intention is expressed. Be sure to appoint a new Guardian under your new Will or make an appointment in a separate document.

Although, as stated above, the funds to support your children will come from your estate initially, the guardian may need to meet some or all the expenses should your estate run out of funds. The other option would be placing the children into highly undesirable care.

Estate/Assets/Property

People often wonder what is meant by their estate because, as far as they are concerned, they do not own a country farm or any great portfolio of assets. When discussing successions, Wills, and probate, we describe all that you own as your estate. This means that if all you own is the shirt on your back, that is your estate. Others may own houses, cars, household items, jewellery, bitcoin, copyright, gold bars, or shares, and that will be their estate.

You should take a few important steps before you start writing your Will. Firstly, you should have a clear idea as to who you want to appoint as your Executor(s) and be able to state their name(s), address(es), and relationship(s) to you. Likewise, regarding who you want to appoint as Guardian(s) if you have minor children for whom you would like to put in place guardianship, be ready to give their proper name(s), address(es), and their relationship(s) to you.

You will also want to consider your worth. This means your assets and liabilities. Do you own those assets outright, or do you own them with someone else? If you own them with someone else, how do you own them: is it as "Joint Tenants" or "Tenants in Common?" The way in which you own property will have a major implication on how you can dispose of it, so this is a must-know. If you have forgotten what the terms "Joint Tenant" and "Tenants in Common" mean, refresh your understanding below and the impact.

Joint Tenants

The concept of jointly held property is puzzling to many. This is because the nature of joint ownership has different legal implications. It is important that you understand how you may hold property jointly with another and the legal implication of the manner of your joint ownership.

When a person says that they own property with another as Joint Tenants, they are saying that all the owners own all of the property, and should one of the owners die, the whole of the property automatically becomes owned by the survivor(s). If, for example, you own a piece of land or a home as Joint Tenants with your partner, it means both of you own the whole, and should one of you die, the whole becomes owned by the survivor. This is really crucial to understand.

To find out how you hold joint property, it is important to check your Deeds or the title documents to the property. You will be sure to find it in there. You will not be free to dispose of your share as you see fit until you have served a "Notice of Severance" on the other party.

Tenants in Common

On the other hand, where the property is held jointly as "Tenants in Common," it means that you own it in shares, and you are free to dispose of your share as you see fit. For example, friends Tom and John agree to purchase a house as

Tenants in Common. If they both chip in and contribute 50% of the price, they will likely own the property 50/50.

Tom may want to get out of the deal in time, perhaps because he has now fallen out of friendship with John, or he needs to travel abroad. Tom would be within his rights to sell his share of the property to Ana. When Tom decides to write his Will, he may dispose of his share as he sees fit in his Will without needing to serve a notice on John. Understanding this type of ownership is, therefore, critical.

Per stirpes

Per stirpes: Sometimes, in your Will, you may want to give a gift to a child or children and pass it on to their children or your grandchildren or their child or children if they are not related to you. In such circumstances, the term "per stirpes" is used as it automatically relays that the gift is to pass to the issue of the person to whom it has been given.

Per capita

Per capita: Where you wish to give a gift to a group of persons but do not wish for that gift to pass on to their issue, but you want the gift to be given to the last person or persons who survive the testator from those in that group, the word "per capita" is used. So if one of your beneficiaries were to pass before you, your estate or the gift would be distributed equally amongst the remaining.

Residue of Your Estate

The "residue of an estate" is the term used to catch any property that has inadvertently not been disposed of under the Will. For example, Tom owns a car, a house, and its contents. He gives his house to John under his Will and the car to Ana; however, he gives the residue of his estate to John. The fact that he gave John the house does not mean that John would automatically be entitled to the contents of the house unless Tom had stated so specifically.

However, in this case, John would still get the contents, as Tom named him as the person who would receive any property he had not disposed of in the Will.

Tip:

The residue is anything left over that you have not gifted.

Domicile[1][1]

This word frightens the most seasoned Will Writers. It simply means your place of permanent residence. As the law of England and Wales is known for its complications, your domicile may be a domicile of origin, a domicile of dependence, or a domicile of choice.

Your domicile of origin usually means the place where you were born. You may be asked about your domicile of choice

– which is the place you have decided to call home and make your permanent residence. A domicile of dependence applies to children who are dependent upon the domicile of their parents or Guardians.

To make matters a bit more complicated, English law also embraces the concept of habitual residence – some of us have homes around the world, and the taxman and the courts sometimes need to take a look at where we habitually reside to determine how to apply the rules of domicile to us. A guiding light in determining domicile in the United Kingdom is whether you have actually resided in the United Kingdom for at least seventeen years of the past twenty years.

Let us not forget as we read this book how Brexit may apply. As Europeans leave Britain because of Brexit, they will eventually lose their domicile of choice in Britain as they return to their domiciles of origin, the places where they were born. Europeans who leave Britain to return to their places of birth will lose Britain as their domicile of choice if they reside out of the United Kingdom for four tax years out of the last twenty. We shall consider the impact - if any - of Brexit as we endeavour to write a tax- efficient Will.

What-if Scenarios

When writing your Will, think within the context of "What if." For example, John is twenty-five years old and has decided to write his Will as he is embarking on global travel for three years with Tom. He hopes to return, but his mom is worried and has advised him to write his Will just in case before he leaves. John wishes to give all his property to his mom should anything happen to him. His mom is now sixty years old. John needs to consider who he would give his property should his mom pass before him.

John thinks long and hard and decides to give all his assets first to his mom, then to his cousin Jeff if she passes before him, and should Jeff pass before him, then to Jeff's son Phil. This enables John to ensure that there is always someone nominated to receive the benefit of his property should he pass. This does not provide any guarantees, but at least John has tried. If they should all pass before John or die in the same event as him, John has named the Dogs Trust – a registered charity in England and Wales – to receive the residue of his estate. Hopefully, the charity will outlive them all.

Change

Life is about change. We start as infants, become teenagers, and grow into adults. Our focus, status, and location change as we move into adulthood. It is therefore important to embrace these changes and consider their impact on your Will.

If you have moved from being single to being married or in a civil partnership, this change in status will impact your Will. If you now have three children or even one child, you need to consider the impact this will have on your Will. If you own a property abroad, it is critical that you understand the impact this may have on your Will. The country where you own property may have its own laws of inheritance. For example, you may be obliged to leave some property to your siblings. It is important that you consider all these things based on your circumstances.

Tip:

Think ahead, expect the best, and plan for the worst.

In this book, we shall examine the journey of Jane Doe, who we will first join while working at a local supermarket but will experience ever-changing circumstances that will require changes to her Will. Her Will is drafted as she goes through life. We shall also discuss the impact of each change on her life and what she needs to consider as her life progresses. Her changing circumstances and how they affect her liability to inheritance tax will be considered.

Will she be able to avoid this death tax? If yes, what will she do to ensure the taxman does not catch her out?

It is always a good idea to identify before writing your Will the people you may wish to appoint as actors in your Will and identify possible replacements should they pass before you. This gives your Will some future- proofing. In order to assist you in doing just that, I have provided a form in Appendix II, which will help you to focus your mind on the people you need to consider appointing in your Will. You will need to be able to give their names, addresses, and relationship to you. You will also need to consider their ages if they are minors or less likely to outlive you.

CHAPTER 3

THE INHERITANCE TAX PROVISIONS

Let us now consider the issue of inheritance tax. At this book's publication date, inheritance tax in the United Kingdom is set at 40%. This is expected to remain so until it is reviewed in 2026.

Tip[2]²:

Inheritance tax in the United Kingdom is 40% of your estate in excess of £325,000, plus any exemptions.

Every person at death currently has a nil rate band of £325,000. This means that if your assets are worth less than £325,000, you are not liable to pay inheritance tax at death. If you are single with no kids and no home, your nil rate band would be £325,000.

An allowance has been granted in relation to your primary residence in the sum of £175,000. Considering that the average home in the UK is priced at around £375,000, this can be considered as half a loaf being better than no bread. This exemption also comes with the conditionality that the home must be passed to your direct descendant. Direct descendants are defined as natural children, step-children of a married couple, or adopted children.

The benefit of the residential nil rate band is lost if your estate is worth in excess of 2 million pounds. This means that the half loaf you were given of £175,000 is taken away by depriving you of £1 for every £2 in value of your estate above £2 million pounds. The outcome achieved is that if your estate is worth £2.35 million, you would have lost the benefit of the residential nil rate band unless some other exemptions apply.

If you are single and with no children and a home, your nil rate band will still be £325,000. You will have the benefit of the residence nil rate band, but you will only be able to use it if you are able to pass it to your child or children. If you are without a direct descendant, you may only be exempted to the tune of £325,000.

If you are single with a child or children, you will have a total nil rate band of £325,000 plus £175,000, giving you a total nil rate band of £500,000. This is £500,000 to pass on tax-free to your kids.

In addition, married partners are both severally entitled to these allowances. This would mean that a couple with no children would be entitled to a joint allowance of £650,000, which they may pass on tax-free. There is a catch, gross advantage to being married as you can transfer any amount of value to each other at 0% inheritance tax.

A married couple or civil partnership with children and a home to pass on to their children would be able to pass a total of £1,000,000.00 to their children, tax-free. You may ask why only £1,000,000.00? This is because although they can pass unlimited value to each other, a cap is placed on them when they intend to pass property to others. One million pounds is all they would be able to pass, tax fee to their kids. This amount comprises the husband's and wife's allowance of £325,000 each plus their residential home allowance of £175,000 each, giving them a total of one million pounds to pass tax-free to their children.

Let's set it out here:

Mum has £325,000 (personal allowance)

Dad has £325,000 (personal allowance)

Main residence allowance to pass on from Mum up to a value of £175,000

Main residence allowance to pass on from Dad up to a value of £175,000

Total benefit to pass to son: £1,000,000.

I can literally hear you asking, does it have to be the same house? No, you have several homes; you or your trustees can designate one as your main residence.

Tip[3]**³:**

Private residence allowance as of 2022- 2026 stands at £175,000.

_____

Combining the personal allowance and residential property nil rate band of both parents enables parents to pass £1,000,000 to their children (tax-free).

In addition to what can be passed to your children tax-free at death, in your lifetime, you may make the following gifts tax-free:

- Small gifts of £250 to as many different people as you wish with no consequence.
- Gifts to UK-registered charities and charities outside the UK (if they meet the same criteria to be registered as a UK charity) if they had been established in the UK.
- A gift of £3,000 to the same person in a tax year.
- Gifts in consideration of marriage:

  → From parents = £5,000

  → From grandparents = £2,500

  → From the marrying parties to each other = £2,500 either way

  → From other relatives = £1,000.

- Gift of any amount of money, once you survive seven years.

Let us explore a few more exemptions, although this is not a finite list.

Gifts between married partners or those in a civil partnership attract 0% inheritance tax.

Gifts to charities and exempt bodies. These bodies need to be registered in the UK or must be bodies that would be recognised as charities in the United Kingdom, the European Union, Iceland, or Norway or be able to meet that criteria if located outside the UK.

Gifts made to social landlords, such as gits to housing associations, are also exempt. The same principles apply to gifts for national purposes, such as national museums and galleries. It stands to reason that national heritage properties should also be offered this exemption. Gifts to political parties fall within this exemption of 0% inheritance tax. An exemption has also been provided for the benefit of our servicemen who die in active service.

If you are filthy rich? There are many of the above exemptions which can be considered. You may also wish to explore securing the services of a tax advisor.

Let us move on to exploring how these provisions may affect you based on your circumstances.

CHAPTER 4

SINGLE, NO KIDS, & BROKE

In Chapter 1, I introduced you to Jane. Jane represents the single male or female with no kids who wishes to write a Will. When we first join her, she has a job at the local supermarket and lives with mum and dad and her cat Felix. Jane lives from day to day, giving little thought to pension, insurance, or savings. She has little or no savings. Her bank account shows a balance of £1,000. Her sister Annie left home five years ago and is married with two lovely boys whom she adores.

One day, Jane gets chatting with her friend Emma, who has lost a family member. Emma's family had not made provisions for inheritance tax or considered any form of estate planning, leaving the remaining family in a position where they are now trying to figure it all out. This really unsettles Jane, who becomes determined to put her affairs in order should the unexpected happen.

These circumstances triggered her thoughts about her own future and wellbeing, and Jane starts thinking about her Will. She decides to leave everything to her mum and dad. They are the most important people in her life and have been there for her at every stage of her life. Then it dawns on her, "What if mum and dad go before me?"

This thought troubles Jane. She knows that it is a real probability that her mom and dad may pass before her. Should her parents predecease her, her gift to them will fail, and she will need to reconsider her Will once they have passed.

She decides to future-proof her Will so that should her mom and dad pass before her, someone will still be nominated to receive her assets. She thinks long and hard about it and decides to benefit her sister Annie and her two adorable nephews should the unthinkable happen and her mum and dad pass before her.

A few days later, Jane runs into Emma again and tells her all about her plan to write her Will. They decide to calculate Jane's net worth, being the value of all that she owes. They tally that Jane's only asset appears to be £1000.00 in the bank, her clothes and shoes at home, which are not branded and would only be of nominal value as second-hand goods on the open market.

Emma tells Jane that she really does not see the need for her to write her Will, as she is only worth £1,000 right now, and her personal items taken together, such as her clothes, may be worth less or about the same. The threshold for the payment of inheritance tax is £325,000, and she is far away from that mark.

Emma understands that her words may hurt Jane and come across as insensitive, but as friends, they have sworn to be honest with each other. Further, Emma informs Jane that from her research, if your estate is worth £5,000 or less, there really is nothing to worry about, as such matters can be dealt with under the rules governing small estates. Emma advises Jane to look it up, telling her that most banks and building societies would be happy to close an account with less than £5,000 once provided with the death certificate by the next of kin.

Jane realises that her estate will qualify as a small estate[4]4 as she only has £1,000 in the bank and nothing more of value. She promises Emma that she will think about her advice.

On the way home from meeting with Emma, Jane stops by the newsagent and plays the Lotto. Jane feels lucky and believes that she may "WIN BIG" one day. Jane also thinks to herself, "What if my parents were to pass and leave me an inheritance?" She recalls the story of the members of the family who were all ill with COVID-19 at the same time and passed within days of each other. This makes her realise that her circumstances could change at any time.

Jane decides to write a Will as a precaution, reasoning that her circumstances could change at any time and there is no harm in having a Will. It would help her feel better and less anxious if she had a Will. The Will would identify who she would want her assets to go to in the event that she inherits any property from her parents or a long-forgotten relative.

In her Will, she would be able to identify who she would like to benefit and not take the risk of her property going to unintended beneficiaries.

Jane does not need to worry about inheritance tax right now as she is well within her nil rate band, which is a tax-free allowance at death. Everyone who dies in 2022 through to 2026 is entitled to a nil rate or zero percent tax band of up to £325,000 plus any exemptions which may apply to them or of which they wish to take advantage before they become eligible to pay the 40% inheritance tax.

She is, however, worried about her cat Felix and decides to make provision for him in the Will. She also wants her family to know the type of funeral she would like. In the United Kingdom, organ donation has become an automatic "opt-in," so it is unnecessary to address this in her Will. If she wanted to opt out, Emma had told her that all she had to do was to go on the www.gov.uk website, search "organ donation," and follow the instructions to opt-out. With all of the above in mind, Jane sets about writing her Will.

Last Will and Testament

I, Jane Doe of 59 Orchard Park, Long View, London OL4 2WX, being of sound mind, make this Will as my Last Will and Testament.

I hereby revoke all former Wills, Codicils, or other Testamentary instruments made by me. This Will applies to all my assets located in England and Wales.

1. I appoint as Executors and Trustees of this my Will my parents, Richard Doe my father, and Pricilla Doe my mother, both of 59 Orchard Park, Long View, London OL4 2WX.

2. Should one or both my parents be unwilling or unable to act, I appoint the survivor of them who is able and willing to act as sole Executor and Trustee of this my Will.

3. In the event that both or neither of my parents are unwilling or unable to act as my Executors and Trustees at the time of my death, I appoint my sister Annie Doe-Blackwell of 40 Sunset Boulevard, London SW1 5RJ as sole Executrix and Trustee of this my Will. In the event that she is unwilling or unable to act, I appoint my cousin Lacy Brown of 50 Acre Close, London SW5 4LJ as Executrix of this my Will.

4. Should all the Executors mentioned above and Trustees predecease me, and John Blackwell has

attained the age of majority, I appoint my nephews Jake and John Blackwell of 40 Sunset Boulevard, London SW1 5RJ as co-Executors and Trustees or the survivor of them.

5. The standard provisions of the Society of Trust and Estate Practitioners (2nd Edition) shall apply to the provisions of this Will.

6. I direct that all my just debts and funeral expenses be paid as soon as conveniently possible after my death.

7. I give, devise, and bequeath all my estate, to my parents in equal shares, namely, to my father Richard Doe of 59 Orchard Park, Long View, London OL4 2WX, and my mother Pricilla Doe, both of the same address.

8. In the event that one of my parents should predecease me, I give all of my estate to the surviving parent.

9. In the event that both my parents should predecease me, I give all of my estate to my sister Annie Doe-Blackwell of 40 Sunset Boulevard, London SW1 5RJ.

10. Should my sister Annie predecease me, I give, devise, and bequeath all of my estate in equal shares, per stirpes, to my two nephews, the sons of my sister Annie Doe-Blackwell, namely Jake and John Blackwell, both of 40 Sunset Boulevard, London SW1 5RJ.

11. In the event that I should predecease my cat Felix, I give Felix to my sister Annie.

12. Should my sister Annie predecease my cat Felix and me, I give Felix the cat to Jake Blackwell of 40 Sunset Boulevard, London SW1 5RJ.

13. I wish to be cremated.

14. The residue of my estate I give to the registered charity "Cats' Lives Matter," Charity Number #20192020, whose registered address is 148 Hatton Cross, London SW1 2HL.

As witness my hand this [*date*] day of [*month*] 202[…]

[*Signature of person whose Will it is*]

Signed by the Testator in our presence and attested by us in the presence of the Testator and each other.

Witness 1:

Name:

Occupation:

Address:

Signature:

Witness 2:

Name:

Occupation:

Address:
Signature:

Jane now feels lighter. She knows that she has accounted for just about every eventuality. She feels assured that if things were to take an unexpected turn and all the family was to pass in the same event, the charity "Cats' Lives Matter" would benefit from her estate. She checked its status with the Charity Commission and confirmed it is a registered charity.

Jane also included the STEP Standard Provisions (2nd Edition) to guide the actions of her trustees in the exercise of their powers.

Some days later, Jane meets Emma and shows her the Will. Emma asks Jane why she stated in the Will that she would appoint Jake and John as co-Executors and Trustees when they would only be able to act together when John reached his majority, in other words, turned eighteen.

Jane explains that if Jake and John needed to act as her Executors, it would mean that all other Executors had predeceased or were unwilling or unable to act. She wanted the two boys to act together since they were the ultimate Beneficiaries, and by acting together, they would be able to support each other and come into their inheritance at the same time. She did not want Jake to be in charge of what belonged to John only because he was already eighteen and

John was not. She felt that ensuring they could only act together when John was eighteen as he was the younger of the two, would enable John to have a say as Executor and Trustee in how the estate was managed. This would reduce conflict between the two lads.

Emma also wants to know what "per stirpes" means – Jane explains that she had found out that if Jake or John were to pass leaving behind children, the gift would pass to their kids. The use of the phrase made it possible for her to benefit the next generation. "Per stirpes" could be thought of as a magic term. It could be used when a parent gives a gift to a child and wants to benefit any grandchildren, or any children her child may have, should the child pass leaving behind children.

Emma tells Jane that it really is not a great idea to leave substantial amounts to her parents, as that property is only likely to be passed down to her and her sister after the passing of her parents. However, as the amount in question is so small, namely Jane's £1,000 in her bank account, it would not impact her parents' financial position. Emma advises Jane to keep her Will under review as her circumstances   change.

THINGS TO CONSIDER

If you are single with no children, your nil rate band is £325,000. You will pay 40% inheritance tax on anything above this that does not qualify for its own exemption.

If you are a single mum or dad with a family home, your nil rate band is £325,000, but you are also entitled to claim a residential nil rate band of £175,000 if you are passing your family home to your child or children.

Your allowance will be £500,000. You will pay 40% inheritance tax on any amount above this, that does not fall within an exemption.

If you are single with less than £5,000 in assets like Jane, you may not need a Will, and your estate can be dealt with as a small estate. There will be no inheritance tax to pay.

There is no harm whatsoever with writing a will, as you never know when you may receive an unexpected windfall.

CHAPTER 5

OUTWIT THE TAXMAN

Jane's discussions with Emma about the value of her estate had left her concerned. She realised she needed to start thinking about her pension, life insurance, and savings. Focusing on these things would help her build her assets. She had been playing the Lotto and had even bought a few scratch cards, but so far, she had won little or nothing. In fact, she had lost more playing than she had won.

The whole COVID-19 experience made her appreciate life and value sharing time with her parents. The lockdown had separated so many families and forced them to protect their loved ones. She, too, had decided to move out of her parents' home during that time as her presence there had placed them at great risk if infection transmitted from her.

She worked at a supermarket and was in regular contact with shoppers who could infect her. To reduce any such possibility, she moved out of her parents' home and got herself a tiny one-bedroom apartment. Taking her cat Felix, she moved out.

The supermarket where she worked decided to provide all staff with "Death in Service Benefit" totaling £100,000 per employee. Jane understood that should she die while employed with the supermarket, her beneficiaries would be entitled to her Death in Service funds. This benefit would only be available to her while she was working at the supermarket. Should she leave her employment with the company, she would no longer be entitled to the Death in Service package.

Jane remembered that the supermarket had also offered a pension plan when she joined, but she had not taken it seriously. She decided to change that approach to her financial wellbeing and understand more about how a pension plan works and how it may benefit her long-term. She enquired with Human Resources about the pension scheme, who provided her with the details. It was growing steadily and was now worth in the region of £40,000.

Jane decided to take a small Life Insurance policy of £250,000. Further, since her last discussion with Emma about the cost of funerals, she had increased her savings from £1,000 to £3,000 at the local bank. She did not want to leave her parents or anyone else in a position where they would have to find the funds to pay for her funeral. Emma had explained to her the financial strain her family had suffered as a result of having to bury family members who themselves had insufficient funds to meet the costs. Emma had informed her that the family members who had not written tax-efficient wills had found themselves having to sell the asset left for their benefit to pay the inheritance tax. This had defeated the whole purpose of the gift left for that family member.

Jane became concerned that her assets were increasing and began to wonder whether she would be liable for inheritance tax. During their conversation, Emma had informed her that there were things her family members could have done to reduce the tax, but they had failed to do so. One such thing was to have ensured that any Life Insurance was written in Trust. This simply means that you name a beneficiary on your life insurance policy.

This would have guaranteed that the amount would pass to the beneficiary outside the estate. Thus, it would not have been included in the inheritance tax calculation, which rendering the value of the estate. She had learnt that at death, estates valued at £325,000 or less would not be subject to this 40% tax. Her estate would need to be valued over this amount for her to be liable to pay the 40% tax on any amount in excess of £325,000.

Jane now knows that her Life Insurance, Death in Service benefit, and Pension plan can pass outside her estate. Thereby reducing the value of her estate for inheritance tax purposes.

Emma had hinted that to ensure that she reduces the value of her estate for inheritance tax, she would have to nominate someone to receive her Death in Service Benefit to guarantee that if she passed while working at the supermarket, it would be paid to the person she had nominated directly. She would also have to do the same with her Life Insurance.

The effect of nominating someone would be twofold. Firstly, the amounts would be written into Trust, meaning that they would be held by that company, to be passed to her nominee at the time of her passing. Secondly, the amount would not be included in her estate, thus reducing the value of her estate and her exposure to inheritance.

Jane did not recall nominating anyone to receive her Death in Service, Pension, or Life Insurance, and Emma strongly advised her to discuss it with the Human Resources department at her place of work. She also advised her to call the insurance and pension company to tell them that she wanted to nominate someone to receive her funds. They would require her to complete a nomination form, which may be available online, or they may post her a hard copy for completion and return to them.

Jane thought all night long about the advice Emma had given her, and on her next day at work, she spoke with the Human Resources manager, who gave her the relevant form to complete. She decided to nominate her sister Annie.

Later that day, she phoned the insurance and pension company, who informed her that the required form was available online. She immediately went online and completed it. The day ended quickly, but she felt that she had achieved much. Her actions would ensure that her Death in Service, Life Insurance, and Pension would not count as part of her estate for the purposes of inheritance tax, as those amounts would now pass to her nominated beneficiaries tax-free.

Now, despite having increased her asset base by nominating beneficiaries for her Death in Service, Life Insurance, and Pension fund, Jane did not have to worry about the 40% inheritance tax liability. She decided to calculate how much tax she had avoided by simply nominating beneficiaries:

Death in Service = £100,000.00
Life Insurance = £250,000.00
Pension = £40,000.00
Savings = £3,000.00
Total Assets = £393,000.00
Less Nil Rate Band = £325,000.00
Amount Subject to 40% Inheritance Tax = £68,000.00

Inheritance Tax Payable 40% of £68,000.00 =**£27,200.00**

However, now that she had nominated persons to receive her Death in Service, her Pension, and her Life Insurance, all of these assets would pass outside of her estate. Instead of worrying about where her executors would find £27,200.00 to pay the inheritance tax liability, she had been able to secure £390,000 to pass outside of her estate, thus benefiting her loved ones more abundantly.

Jane still had her nil rate band of £325,000.00. The only bit that would be considered as part of her estate would be the

£3,000 in her bank account. This left her with £322,000, which she could build up to benefit her loved ones.

Jane was now stress-free. Her taxable asset was only her savings of £3,000, which were well within the £325,000 tax-free inheritance tax threshold. She had saved her Executors the worry of an inheritance tax bill of **£27,200** by dealing with her Death in Service, Life Insurance, and Pension, as Emma had advised her.

Knowing that she did not have to worry about inheritance tax, should she pass any day now, Jane relaxed and focused on enjoying life.

Tip:

Nominate Beneficiaries for your Death in Service, Life Insurance, and Pension funds.

THINGS TO CONSIDER

Write into Trust:

1. *Your Pension*

2. *Death in Service benefit*

3. *Your Life Insurance*

Your nominated Beneficiary will receive these sums tax-free as it is not considered part of your estate. If it is not in Trust, it will pass into your estate, and you will pay 40% inheritance tax on any amounts in excess of £325,000 unless additional exemptions apply.

CHAPTER 6

LIVING TOGETHER

A few days later, Jane was at work, on duty at checkout, when their eyes met. They exchanged glances, and without realising, she blushed. They started chatting as she passed his items through the scanner. He asked her how her day was going, adding that he had been admiring her as he stood in the queue. He told her his name was Frank and asked when she was finishing her shift. Jane felt flutters in her stomach as she responded that she would be free at 5 p.m. He asked if she would have a drink with him after work, and she agreed. From that moment, she could not get him out of her mind.

Five o'clock came, and she wondered if he would be there as she exited the store, but he was waiting for her there. They spent the rest of the evening chatting at the local café across the street and agreed to meet the following evening. Things moved quickly; before long, she had introduced Frank to her parents, and he had introduced her to his. They spent Christmas together that year and started imagining how wonderful it would be to start a life together.

Frank moved in with Jane. They enjoyed each other's company and visited many wonderful World Heritage sites together. Then one day, Jane started to dream about starting a family with Frank. She mentioned her feelings to Frank, whose reaction was a bit confusing, as he simply replied, "Maybe one of these days," and showed no enthusiasm.

Frank's reaction confused Jane, so she decided to have a chat with Emma about it. They met at the local café later that week, and Jane explained to Emma how she had been thinking of having kids. Her biological clock was ticking, and her hormones were now causing her to think about it more than ever. She had mentioned it to Frank, who seemed disinterested in the topic.

As they sat there having a light snack, she asked Emma whether she knew anything about how having kids with Frank might affect her, as they were not married or in a civil partnership.

Emma explained that one of her relatives had passed recently and had been living with her partner for five years. They had not put a Will in place before he passed, and she had found herself not automatically entitled to any of his property. His property had been inherited by his family members and distributed amongst his siblings, as his parents had predeceased him.

She had been advised that she could make a claim upon his estate for maintenance, as he had paid all the bills and saw to her needs, but as she did not have the funds to pay for a lawyer to represent her and did not want to be a bother, she had simply moved on with her life.

She stated that she would have made such an application under the Inheritance (Provision for Family and Dependents) Act 1975 had there been children in the relationship. She had met all the relevant criteria as they had been cohabiting or living together as if they were husband and wife for two years before his passing. It had been really hard leaving with nothing, as she had spent so many years with him only to walk away empty-handed.

Jane felt really sad to hear about Emma's relative and the fact that she had received no automatic protection under the law and would have had to bring a legal claim under the Inheritance (Provision for Family and Dependents) Act 1975, as a Will had not been written to make provision for her.

Emma warned Jane to think carefully about leaving herself vulnerable as a co-habiting partner. Jane thought to herself that she really did not want to end up like that. She would want Frank to protect her interest and that of any children they may have by writing a Will to make provision for her and the children or marry her, thereby giving her an entitlement should anything happen to him.

Jane realised that there were several benefits that married couples or those in civil partnerships enjoy above and beyond the legal provisions for those cohabiting. It also concerned her that Frank had not been too enthusiastic about having children when she had last spoken with him. She made up her mind to lay the matter to rest and to take her relationship with Frank one day at a time until they were both on the same page about this issue.

THINGS TO CONSIDER

Living together with someone for two years or more does not entitle you to an automatic share of their estate. To secure an entitlement, your partner will need to write a Will providing for you, or you will need to make a claim under the Inheritance (Provision for Family and Dependents) Act 1975 should your partner predecease you, leaving no Will.

CHAPTER 7

CONTEMPLATION OF MARRIAGE

Not long after, Jane informed Emma that Frank had posed the big question, and she had said, "Yes." Emma was happy for Jane, as she could see that Jane was so smitten with Frank's love, and it appeared to her that Jane had found her soulmate.

The date was set for 15 July, and Jane was busy making wedding arrangements. Emma was to be her "Maid of Honour" and her darling nephews Jake and John Blackwell to be her page boys. Jane was ever so excited. The guest list had to be kept to the minimum as social distancing had to be complied with. This limited their guest list to family and friends.

As Jane became increasingly excited about her upcoming wedding and her new life with Frank, she wondered how it would affect the Will she had written. She had learnt from Emma that her marriage to Frank would result in the automatic revocation of her former Will and that she would need to write a new one once she and Frank were married.

Emma had informed her that she had heard that people could make a Will in contemplation of marriage. If she did that, she would not need to write another Will after the wedding, as the Will written in contemplation of marriage would remain valid. To make a Will in contemplation of marriage, all you need is the details of the person you are contemplating marrying. This excited Jane. She wanted to update her Will immediately by revoking the old Will and writing a new Will in contemplation of her marriage to Frank.

Last Will and Testament

I, Jane Doe of 59 Orchard Park, Long View, London OL4 2WX, being of sound mind, make this Will in contemplation of marriage to Frank Rosenberg, of 70 Chequers Lane, Gravesend, London SW1 5RJ as my Last Will and Testament.

I hereby revoke all former Wills, Codicils, or other Testamentary instruments made by me. This Will applies to my property in England and Wales.

1. I appoint as sole Executor and Trustee of this my Will, my husband-to-be Frank Rosenberg, of 70 Chequers Lane Gravesend, London SW1 5RJ, should he survive me by 30 days.

2. In the event that my husband-to-be predeceases me or is unwilling or unable to act, I appoint my sister Annie Doe-Blackwell of 40 Sunset Boulevard, London SW1 5RJ as Executrix of this my Will.

3. In the event that my sister Annie Doe-Blackwell is unwilling or unable to act, and her son John Blackwell has attained the age of majority, I appoint her two sons, Jake and John Blackwell, as co-Executors and Trustees of this my Will or the survivor of them.

4. I direct that all my just debts and funeral expenses be paid as soon as convenient after my death.

5. I give all of my estate to my husband-to-be, Frank Rosenberg, should he survive me by 30 days, failing which I give, devise, and bequeath all of my estate to my sister Annie Doe-Blackwell of 40 Sunset Boulevard, London SW1 5RJ.

6. Should my sister Annie Doe-Blackwell predecease my husband-to-be Frank Rosenberg and me leaving behind children who survive her, I give, devise, and bequeath all of my estate in equal shares, per stirpes, to my two nephews Jake and John Blackwell, both of 40 Sunset Boulevard, London SW1 5RJ, or any of their offspring who may survive me at the time of my death, upon attaining the age of 18 years.

7. I wish to be cremated.

8. Should my cat Felix survive, I wish that he be cared for by my nephew Jake Blackwell of 40 Sunset Boulevard, London SW1 5RJ.

9. The residue of my estate I give, devise, and bequeath to the registered charity "Cats' Lives Matter," Charity Number #20192020, whose registered address is 148 Hatton Cross, London SW1 2HL.

As witness my hand this [*date*] day of [*month*] 202[…]
[*Signature of person whose Will it is*]

Signed by the Testator in our presence and attested by us in the presence of the Testator and each other.

Witness 1:	
Name:	
Occupation:	
Address:	
Signature:	

Witness 2:	
Name:	
Occupation:	
Address:	
Signature:	

The day finally came. The ceremony was conducted at the local Registry Office in Orchard Park. The honeymoon had been planned as a week at the Glen Morgan Hotel, a luxury resort located just outside the city centre. They had made every effort to try to stay safe, which meant avoiding international travel. Their suite at the hotel was absolutely splendid, and Jane looked forward to their first night together as husband and wife.

The wedding ceremony had taken place at midday that day. This had allowed them sufficient time to get to Glen Morgan by 6 p.m. that day to start their honeymoon. That evening, they had dinner in the hotel's gourmet dining restaurant. Jane was ever so happy. She could not recall ever having felt so joyful before and feeling such love, save from her cat Felix.

Dinner ended at about 10 p.m. as they chatted about nothing in particular, just the little mishaps of the day. Jane took in the splendour and grandeur of the place. The manicured gardens, the floral arrangements, and the many fountains of love create that perfect atmosphere.

Jane was having such a wonderful time. However, on Wednesday, she got into a row with Frank over her cat Felix sleeping in the bed. Frank had always objected to Felix sharing the bed with them and had gotten Jane to promise that she would restrict the cat once they were married. However, Jane argued that she could not understand why he was so "hung up" about Felix sharing the bed with them. She would be willing to keep the cat out of the bed if there was a child, but they had planned to delay having children until they had improved their savings and bought their own place.

That evening, the atmosphere at the dinner table was tense. Frank seemed withdrawn, but Jane tried to ignore it. After dinner, Frank asked to be excused. He said he wanted to check on something in the bedroom and would be back shortly, as Jane wanted to sit a little longer in the lounge. He kissed her lovingly on her left cheek and left to go upstairs to the bedroom.

Jane was unconcerned and simply awaited his return. The minutes passed, and it was soon one hour since he had left. Frank had not returned. Jane started to get worried and decided to go upstairs to the bedroom to check on him. She entered the bedroom, hoping to find that he had fallen asleep due to exhaustion and the day's excitement. Frank, however, was not there.

Her concern turned to anxiety, and she became frantic as she checked the bedroom and bathroom. She also noticed that his suitcase was gone. She decided to call his mobile. The phone rang off. A few minutes later, she received a WhatsApp message which read: *"Am sorry dear, I just did not know how to tell you."* Jane never saw or heard from Frank again after that day.

THINGS TO CONSIDER

If you are contemplating marriage, you can write your Will in contemplation of marriage, as a marriage will revoke any Will made prior to marriage.

You must know the name of the person you intend to marry; otherwise, the Will is of no effect. Hopefully, that person will also be looking forward to tying the knot with   you.

CHAPTER 8

THE DIVORCE

Jane was grateful to have friends like Emma. Emma was there to comfort her through such a difficult time. However, she was determined to break through and find positives out of such a negative set of circumstances. She knew that she would need to get a divorce. Emma had informed her that divorce would not revoke her Will, but any gifts or appointments she had made to Frank would fail. It was what Emma told her afterwards that really got her to act quickly.

Emma told her that the nil rate band –currently £325,000 – would be transferrable between her and Frank. Frank could claim her nil rate band if she failed to divorce him and died before him. That really got Jane thinking. She did not want Frank to be able to benefit from her after his behaviour. She also wanted to allow herself the opportunity to start over and find the right person for her. She knew that if she were to get divorced, Frank would not be able to make use of her nil rate band.

However, the transferrable nature of her nil rate band could be applied to a new relationship upon remarriage. The ability to transfer her nil rate band between herself and her spouse tax-free would be beneficial to her and her new family. She did not want to leave it at the mercy of being used by Frank due to her lack of action. By getting a divorce, she could free herself of him and preserve her transferrable nil rate band.

Jane thought it best to rewrite her Will and blot out the name and memory of Frank from it. She filed for a divorce, which Frank did not challenge. Once the "Decree Nisi" and "Decree Absolute" came through, Jane drowned her sorrows in her work. The only consolation was that she did not have to cross paths with Frank daily. He had moved out of the area. He had not even returned to collect the rest of his things.

She had dropped them off for him with his parents, who were disappointed at how things had turned out but did not want to get involved. They had informed her that they had not heard from him for a while, but he did call now and then to say that he was "OK" and insisted on not discussing the matter with them.

Jane did her best to put the matter behind her. She was grateful that they had not had children and that she could walk away without putting a child through such hurt and disappointment.

She focused on her work and improving her bank balance. She planned to save to invest in a home in Spain or the South of France. She had always wanted to buy a holiday home on the continent, in Spain, France, or Portugal. She had now been able to save some £10,000 by putting in overtime. The prevalence of COVID-19 had assisted her saving objective, as going out was less of an option, and she just wanted to focus on accomplishing her dreams.

Now that her divorce was official, Jane set about writing a new Will. The value of her estate was well within her nil rate band of £325,000, but it was hers and hers alone, and the divorce had freed her from the possibility of Frank being able to use it, should she pass before him while they were separated but not divorced. She breathed a sigh of relief as she held the Decree Absolute in her hand and commenced a new   Will.

Last Will and Testament

I, Jane Doe of 59 Orchard Park, Long View, London OL4 2WX, being of sound mind, make this Will as my Last Will and Testament.

I hereby revoke all former Wills, Codicils, or other Testamentary instruments made by me. This Will relates to all my assets located in England and Wales.

1. I appoint my sister Annie Doe-Blackwell of 40 Sunset Boulevard, London SW1 5RJ as sole Executrix of this my Will.

2. In the event that my sister Annie should predecease me or is unwilling or unable to act, and her son John Blackwell has attained the age of majority, I appoint her sons, my nephews, Jake Blackwell and John Blackwell, both of 40 Sunset Boulevard, London SW1 5RJ, to act jointly in her stead or the survivor of them.

3. The standard provisions of the Society of Trust and Estate Practitioners (2nd Edition) shall apply to the provisions of this Will.

4. I direct that all my just debts and funeral expenses be paid as soon as reasonably practicable after my death.

5. I give all of my estate to my sister Annie Doe-Blackwell of 40 Sunset Boulevard, London SW1 5RJ.

6. In the event that she should predecease me, I give, devise, and bequeath in equal shares all of my estate, per stirpes, to my nephews, Jake Blackwell and John Blackwell, both of 40 Sunset Boulevard, London SW1 5RJ, upon attaining the age of 18 years.

7. I wish to be cremated.

8. Should my cat Felix survive me, I wish that he be given to my nephew Jake Blackwell of 40 Sunset Boulevard, London SW1 5RJ.

9. I give the residue of my estate to the registered charity "Cats' Lives Matter," Charity Number #20192020, whose registered address is 148 Hatton Cross, London SW1 2HL.

Signed by me in witness whereof this [*date*] day of [*month*] 202[…] [*signature of Jane Doe*]

Signed by the Testator and attested by us, as witnesses, in the presence of the Testator and of each other.

Witness 1:
Name:
Occupation:
Address:
Signature:

Witness 2:	
Name:	
Occupation:	
Address:	

THINGS TO CONSIDER

If you are estranged from a husband or wife, consider whether it is in your best interests to divorce that partner. It may be advantageous to remain married and use their nil rate band should they pass before you.

However, if you intend to remarry, it is best to get a divorce and enjoy the benefit of a combined nil rate band and residual nil rate band with your new partner, as this will make available the potential to pass £1,000,000 to any children tax-free.

CHAPTER 9

JANE IS APPOINTED AS AN ATTORNEY BY HER PARENTS UNDER THEIR LASTING POWER OF ATTORNEY

Jane became worried about her parents. They were aging, and it was becoming apparent that they would need assistance with handling their daily affairs. She decided to have a chat with Emma about their failing health. She wanted to know what she could do to assist them with managing their social care and financial affairs but did not know how to go about it.

They met that day after work at the local café outside Jane's place of work. This little café had been the location of many of their profound discussions and life-changing decisions. This was where they could sit down and have a one-to-one or heart-to-heart chat.

Emma asked Jane if she had ever heard about Lasting Powers of Attorney. She explained that a Lasting Power of Attorney was in two parts: one focuses on the donor's financial decisions and the other deals with health and care decisions. She advised her to consider doing both as her parents would need both as they age. Now is the best time for them to put these in place, as they still have the mental capacity to make decisions for themselves. Emma encouraged Jane to discuss getting persons appointed to assist them in their decision as soon as possible. They would still maintain control over their affairs, but a document would be in place to show who had been given authority to assist them in arriving at such decisions should the need arise.

Emma directed her to a gov.uk website where she could assist her parents with logging on and completing the forms after they had discussed it. There was also the option to print the forms and complete them. Residents of the UK can access the necessary information at: https://www.gov.uk/government/publications/make-a-lasting-power-of-attorney

The form requires her parents (donor) to appoint Attorneys to attend to their financial matters as well as their health and care decisions. Those appointed can be specified as acting jointly or severally. The form also provides for persons to be notified of the appointment of the Attorney or Attorneys. Jane considered that she and her sister Annie could be appointed to act jointly to care for their parents as they age. Her parents can also include their preferences and give instructions in the form.

The form also requires a Certificate Provider. Jane did not understand what this was or meant. Emma explained that the Certificate Provider must be a person who can assess and confirm that her parents appointed an Attorney(s) of their own free will and were not under any duress to do so. They understood what they were doing.

There are also certain criteria that the Certificate Provider must meet. That person must certify that, as far as they are aware, at the time of signing the form, the donor understood the purpose of the LPA and the scope of the authority conferred under it. That no fraud or undue pressure is being used to induce the donor to create the LPA. There is nothing else that would prevent the LPA from being created by the completion of the instrument.

The Certificate provider must be 18 years or over. He or she must affirm that he/she has read the Lasting Power of Attorney and that nothing prevents him/her from acting as the Certificate Provider. The donor has chosen that person to act as the Certificate provider as someone they have known for two years or more, or the donor has chosen the Certificate Provider as a person with relevant professional skills and expertise.

All this was news to Jane, but she was happy that she now had all the information she needed to find out more as Emma had provided her with the gov.uk link. Jane found out later that a fee was also to be paid for registering the Lasting Power of Attorney. This fee is currently set at £82.00 and should be paid to the Court of Protection in relation to each Lasting Power of Attorney applied for.

Jane felt so much better now. She decided to phone up her sister Annie. She wanted them to discuss the matter together with their parents. Jane realised at that moment that one is never too young or old to have a Lasting Power of Attorney in place. You never know when it will come in handy should you become unwell and unable to manage your affairs. The donor never loses control of their affairs, and the Attorney can act only as instructed by the donor. Jane knew that her parent would be relieved to know that appointing an Attorney did not mean they would be giving up control of their lives and finances. Instead, they would be putting in place the framework for managing their circumstances should the need arise.

As she thanked Emma for her assistance and they parted company, it occurred to her that her parents may not have a Will. She could also use her next meeting with them to discuss the status of their Wills. She felt uncomfortable about having to discuss such matters with them, but she knew it was necessary. She also wanted them to consider how the inheritance tax provisions apply to them and how they might be able to write a tax-efficient will.

CHAPTER 10

GETS A WINDFALL

Once the Decree Absolute came through, Jane drowned her sorrows in her work. The only consolation was that she did not have to cross paths with Frank daily. He had moved out of the area.

Later that year, Jane discovered that Uncle Todd had left her a financial windfall of £400,000. Uncle Todd was her mum's brother, who lived in the Midlands. She had visited him a few times as a child, but they had lost contact, and it had been a while since she had last seen him. He was several years older than her mum and had lived alone with his dog Destiny. Uncle Todd had always been fond of Jane and had treated her like the daughter he never had.

They had found out about his passing from his Solicitor and the Executors of his estate. Luckily, uncle Todd had a Will and had appointed his Solicitor as his Executors and Trustees. He had given them her parents' address as the address of his next of kin, which enabled them to trace her and his family easily. They had not known that he had been unwell. The news of his passing had certainly come as a surprise.

The funeral was a sombre affair. Her mum had taken it hard as Todd had always been like a father to her. She had taken the need to put her affairs in order more seriously by getting their Will done and their Lasting Powers of Attorney.

This unexpected benefit from Uncle Todd left Jane wondering how this may affect her Will, as her assets were now well above the nil rate band of £325,000. She rehearsed her position in her head: She had nominated a beneficiary for her Pension fund, Life Insurance, and Death in Service benefit.

These funds would pass to her beneficiaries outside her estate. This meant that the taxman would not consider them when determining the value of her estate. Prior to this windfall, her assets were well within the nil rate band. With this windfall, she needed to do more to protect herself from the taxman's grasp.

She decided to add up the current value of her estate now that she had received this windfall:

From Uncle Todd = £400,000.00
Savings = £10,000.00
Total Value of Estate = £410,000.00
Less Her Nil Rate Band = -£325,000.00
Taxable Estate = £85,000.00

Inheritance Tax 40% of £85,000.00 = **£34,000.00**

Having worked it all out, Jane knew that if she did not want to pay any tax should something happen to her, she had to consider her options as to how best to dispose of the £85,000 to remain within her nil rate band. Here follows a list of the possibilities she considered:

1. One option was to gift the funds to a local charity. Gifts to charities were exempt gifts. Jane wanted to make provision for cats, especially her cat Felix, should she predecease him. She considered donating to the local Cats Trust, "Cats' Lives Matter."

2. She then considered making use of her Lifetime Exemptions – every year, she has an annual exemption of £3,000, which is tax-free. She could give a gift of £1,500 to each of her nephews, Jake and John, on their birthdays. She believed that by doing this over the next twenty-eight years, she would be able to reduce her net worth and set herself back on track to pay no inheritance tax. Although this was an option, it would take a long time and rely upon the assumption that her assets would not increase over that period.

3. Jane also considered giving the entire amount away to her sister Annie immediately but realised that she would need to survive seven years to ensure that it would be free from inheritance tax. She was young, with no ailments, so surviving seven years was a real possibility.

4. Jane considered giving the funds to her parents. She would have to survive seven years. In any event, if they predeceased her, she may only be increasing

their estate for inheritance tax purposes. Their estate would most likely be passed to her and her sister Annie, meaning they would have to pay the 40% tax should her parents' assets exceed £1,000,000.00. She was not sure of their current net worth, but he knew she would have to give it some thought.

5. Jane knew that many people were struggling to cope with the economic conditions, rising energy prices and inflation at this time, so she thought that maybe she could do something to help. She recalled that her small gift exemption allowed her to make unlimited small gifts of £250 to different people. She gave it some thought. This would mean that she could benefit 340 families struggling at this time while freeing herself of the thought of an inheritance tax burden should she pass anytime soon.

6. Alternatively, she could start treating herself with the excess cash and take a few cruises, vacations, or trips, using up the £85,000 while creating wonderful memories with her loved ones. The only thing was that it was no longer safe to go anywhere during the height of the pandemic.

7. She could put the £85,000 into her Pension pot, as that had already been assigned to a nominated Beneficiary, who would receive it tax-free. Contributions to Pension pots are usually capped annually, so she would need to check. She last

recalled that it had been capped at £40,000[5] annually. This option would take her two to three years to rid herself of the taxable amount.

There was just so much for her to think about. She felt like she needed some time out to make up her mind. She was glad that she could take the time to think it through.

Having considered all these options, Jane decided to put £20,000 into her Pension, as that would come in handy at retirement if she lived to a ripe old age.

She would give £10,000 to her parents to treat themselves to a new kitchen or whatever they fancied. This amount would not adversely increase their estate, and a new kitchen was well overdue.

She would give £50,000 to her sister Annie to use for the benefit of her two sons or in whatever way she felt it could benefit her family. Jane knew that Annie was saving up to buy a new home for her family, so her contribution would be greatly appreciated. She also wanted to see her two nephews having the best life possible and was happy to be in a position to assist.

All she had to do now was survive the next seven years. She noted the date of her gifts to her parents and her sister to ensure that she was fully aware of the date and when the seven years would end. She also wanted to ensure that should she pass within the seven years, her Executors would know when the gifts were made and receive any tapered relief from inheritance tax available.

The remaining £5,000 she would use to benefit those who needed help around her. She could achieve this by making small gifts of £250 and using her annual gift exemption of £3,000.[6][6]

The decision had been hard, but there was no right or wrong in whatever decision she made. The important thing was to dispose of the funds before death in a manner that would not subject her to inheritance tax at death. In any event, she welcomed the opportunity to benefit her parents and her sister in her lifetime. Jane set about transferring the funds to her parents, her sister Annie, and those in need around her.

Jane realised from this experience the importance of having a Will even when you think you have little or nothing. Life is dynamic, and you really never know when you may come into an inheritance or a windfall.

THINGS TO CONSIDER

It is often said that if your net worth is less than £5,000, you need not write a Will, as your estate will be administered as a small estate. However, if there is any possibility that you could come into a windfall or an inheritance, I would advise you to have a Will.

CHAPTER 11

JANE REMARRIES

Everything was going well for Jane. It was the first time since her divorce that she had felt free from the horror of marrying Frank. She was now able to laugh about it. She was younger then, believing in fairy tales of love and romance. Now she was happy with who she was, felt sorry for Frank, was able to forgive him, and wished him well. She realised that the peace she now had was more precious than living in an unhappy relationship.

Then one day, he said hello. She was just having lunch with Emma when he came in. She could not take her eyes off him. He introduced himself as Edward. They exchanged numbers, and this time, she took it slowly. She wanted to get to know him better and did not want her past experience with Frank to get in the way.

It turned out that he was an engineer working with a well-established firm in the city. He had no kids and was interested in starting a family. He believed in the existence of God but was not religious, although he claimed to be most closely affiliated with the Anglican Church. She wanted to get to know as much as possible about him to ensure their compatibility. So far, she had been able to keep her excitement under control, but Edward soon popped the question. Once again, Jane said yes.

This time, however, she did not consider writing a Will in contemplation of marriage as she had done with Frank. However, she wanted to understand how being married could improve her inheritance tax position. She arranged a meeting with Emma.

Emma informed her that transfers of property made between spouses are generally exempt. Jane found this incredible and asked if she was sure. Emma was certain of it. Jane listened carefully as Emma explained some of the benefits of being married or in a civil partnership. If Edward was to pass first and pass all his property to her as a spouse, then there would be no tax to be paid by her. The same would apply if she passed first and left all her property to Edward. No tax would have to be paid.

Emma stated that although transfers between spouses were exempt, they would need to plan carefully when deciding what they could transfer to their children to avoid inheritance tax. She explained that the nil rate band, currently at £325,000, was transferrable between spouses.

This meant that between her and Edward, they would now have the advantage of £650,000 before being liable to pay inheritance tax. This pleased Jane. She had found out that Edward had some savings of his own, a Pension plan, Life Insurance, and Death in Service benefit, for which she had advised him to nominate Beneficiaries.

Now that they were getting married, they both needed to review their nominations. They may now wish to consider nominating each other. Jane considered that as transfers between her and Edward were exempt anyway, they could use their nominations to benefit other family members further down the line tax-free, such as their children.

Jane did not want to change her nominations immediately. She wanted to see how things would work out with Edward and decided that once she was more confident about the trajectory of their relationship, she would reconsider her nominations. The use of their nil rate bands was only necessary for determining how much they could pass down to others tax-free or to their future children before being liable to the 40% inheritance tax.

Emma told her about the residence nil rate band, which was set at £175,000.[7] Each spouse was entitled to it, and it was also transferrable between spouses.

Together, they started working out how much Emma could pass to her children if she and Edward were to pass, leaving children behind. They would have the benefit of £325,000 from Jane's nil rate band and £325,000 from Edward's nil rate band, giving them a total of £650,000.

The government had given each parent the right to pass on £175,000 value, in a property that was their main residence. Each parent was able to pass that amount to the children. In circumstances where the parents were married or in a civil partnership, that residence nil rate band was transferrable between spouses. This meant they could have £175,000 each, giving them a combined total of £350,000, which could be passed to their children.

Their combined nil rate band and residential home allowance would give them a total of £1,000,000 to be transferred to the children before the 40% tax was applied to anything above £1,000,000.

This news made Jane feel happy and hopeful. She understood that as part of a married couple, she would be better able to insulate herself from the 40% inheritance tax regime. What she needed to do, however, was to win Edward over to the idea that they needed to write Wills to protect themselves and secure their children's future.

Emma advised Jane to get further advice, as she had heard that the residence nil rate band could be lost if the value of your estate was to rise beyond £2,000,000. Once the value of an estate rose above £2,000,000, the residence nil rate band benefit would be tapered off and eventually lost, creating a greater tax liability. The tapering is applied at a rate of £1 for every £2 by which the estate exceeds £2,000,000.

The result is that the benefit may be lost totally if your estate exceeds £2,350,000. Where a property is subject to a mortgage, only the equity value of the residence nil rate band can be claimed and it is not possible to assign the value of the residential nil rate band in the same manner that one may assign the value of the nil rate band to a beneficiary. Jane knew that her combined assets with Edward did not surpass £2,000,000, but she was grateful for Emma's advice.

THINGS TO CONSIDER

If you are married, have you taken advantage of your combined nil rate bands (£650,000), plus your combined residence nil rate bands (£350,000), and any business property relief (100% for qualifying businesses) or agricultural property relief (100% for qualifying properties) if you are into farming?

If you do not qualify for 100%, you may be awarded 50%. There are no guarantees; aim for 100% but expect to wrangle with the taxman as he tries to take a piece of your pie.

Remember that if the value of your estate is above £2,000,000, you are likely to lose your residence nil rate band if the value surpasses £2.35 million.

If   possible,   live   modestly.

CHAPTER 12

MARRIED WITH KIDS

Now that Jane had tied the knot again, she focused on making it work and doing her best for herself and her family. She had done her best for her parents and sister Annie, but now she needed to focus on creating a warm and loving home for herself and Edward.

Jane wasted no time. She hinted to him about writing a Will, and he seemed OK with the proposal. They discussed what they wanted to occur should anything happen to them and made some notes. Both wished that should anything happen to either of them before they had kids, they would want their assets to be divided equally between the two families. Edward provided a list of names on his side who he would want to benefit, and Jane provided a list of names on her side.

They were soon no longer worrying about those lists, as Jane began to feel unwell most mornings, only to go on to provide a positive pregnancy test. She was elated.

Edward was more excited than her; he started to ramble on about making arrangements for university and grandchildren when all she had in her hand was a positive pregnancy test. Alarmingly, he also started to discuss the next child, saying that it was best to have them all at once, one after the other, to allow them to grow up together. All in all, they were both happy, and their joy could not be contained.

Soon, baby Eric was welcomed, and soon after that came baby Lisa. They both decided they could not wait any longer to write their Wills. So much had happened in the past three years since their marriage. They had bought a house in the leafy suburbs of Richmond, London, as tenants in common, as each had contributed 50% of the cost.

The property was valued at £1,500,000. They had both contributed significantly to the deposit and wanted to establish themselves in an area where they could take advantage of the outdoors. They ensured that the property was duly registered as a tenancy in common in their respective shares. This would mean that they would each own half the house.

Their relationship had grown from strength to strength, and Jane was certain that Edward was there for the long haul. He had doted on her, and the children had brought great joy to him.

It was now time to consider what they would do about their Wills. They arranged a visit to the Solicitors, who advised them to consider "Mirror Wills." These are Wills where the couple does exactly the same thing with their property, but each has a separate Will. Each party is at liberty to change the terms of their Will, but it can work well where there is love and trust and allows great flexibility for a surviving spouse to adjust to changing circumstances.

They decided to proceed with Mirror Wills. Jane would pass all her property to Edward should he survive her, and Edward would do the same, resulting in 0% tax on the death of the first to die.

They would also appoint each other as sole Executor and Trustee in the first instance so that the survivor would administer the estate. If they were to pass while the children were still minors, they appointed Annie as Guardian of the children in the first instance, and Edward's younger brother Paul Mark only if Annie was unwilling or unable to act as Guardian.

The Solicitor explained that they could choose up to four persons to act as Executors and Trustees in their absence.

Jane explained that she was uncomfortable with the children inheriting the property at age eighteen. The Solicitor explained that she could extend the age of inheritance to any age she preferred. Although the law in England and Wales allowed children to hold property at the age of eighteen, that law could be excluded in the Will to allow them to inherit at Jane's preferred age.

If they were to pass before the 18th birthday of the children, the law allowed for the creation of a statutory trust for the children, commonly referred to as a "0-18- Trust." The law also gives favourable treatment to an "18-25- year Trust," as many parents are uncomfortable with their children inheriting at eighteen or before their 25th birthday.

Jane and Edward decided to allow the children to inherit at age twenty-five and apply the same age of inheritance to their grandchildren. They hoped that the children and grandchildren would learn the value of work and money before coming into their inheritance.

They chose, as their Executors and Trustees, Paul Mark, Edward's brother of 70 Skyline Close, London SW1 2LJ, to act with Annie, Jane's sister, Annie Doe- Blackwell, of 40 Sunset Boulevard, London SW1 5RJ, and Annie's cousin Lacy Brown of 50 Acre Close, London SW5 4XZ.

The Solicitor explained that the Trustees may appoint professionals to assist them in carrying out their duties and that any fees would be deducted from the estate. He also explained the power of Trustees to hold the property on Trust for Sale, with additional powers to postpone the sale, accumulate income, and apply capital and income for the benefit of the children. Further, they could write a "Letter of Wishes" to guide the Trustees on how they would like them to manage the needs of the children. They confirmed they were happy to proceed on that basis and with that understanding.

He drew to their attention the fact that there is no inheritance tax to be paid by a Bereaved Minors Trust (covering the ages of nought to eighteen), but some tax would have to be paid in relation to an 18–25-Trust, at which age, the beneficiaries, would come into their entitlement and the property would exit the Trust.[8][8]

Generally, tax is charged when assets are placed into the Trust at 20%, when assets come out of the Trust at 4.2%, and at the ten-year anniversary of the Trust.

The ten-year anniversary charge would be avoided as the Trust would only run for seven years after their eighteenth birthday.

He confirmed their desire to benefit their grandchildren. This meant should Eric or Lisa predecease them leaving children, they desired that the child left behind (their grandchild) should receive the portion which would have passed to Eric or Lisa. This meant that the Solicitor would declare the gifts to be "per stirpes," which is the technical term used in a Will when a gift is to benefit the children or children of a beneficiary who has passed before the Testator leaving behind a child or children.

Jane and Edward hoped they would both live to see the day of their children's graduation from university. They were only preparing for possibilities in the hope that they would never happen.

They also made provision to address the unlikely event that they should all pass in the same event to benefit Annie's sons, Jake Blackwell and John Blackwell, both of 40 Sunset

Boulevard, London SW1 5RJ. They arranged for any residue to benefit their favourite charity, "Cats' Lives Matter."

As they had not changed the nominations for their Death in Service, Pension plans, and Life Insurance, the Solicitor advised them to consider changing the nominations now to hold the property in Trust for the benefit of Eric and Lisa. This would afford them the advantage of those assets passing outside their estate. This would reduce the value of their estate for the purpose of inheritance tax.

As the assets were passing outside the estate, Eric and Lisa could benefit from age eighteen or over unless the funds were assigned to a separate Trust Fund to administer them, usually referred to as a "Relevant Property Trust." Funds in such Trusts are treated as existing outside the estate of the deceased.

He explained that relevant property trusts were great at protecting children from gold diggers, etc., as they were discretionary trusts. Although the trustee could make a decision to benefit the beneficiary, the beneficiary had no ownership of the assets in the Trust, as they belonged to the Trust. However, there would be charges to be incurred in relation to such a Trust for assets going in, coming out, and at the tenth anniversary.

For the time being, they decided to proceed with the children inheriting those benefits at eighteen, should they pass, before their eighteenth birthday, but they would keep the matter under review.

They set about writing their Mirror Wills as follows:

Last Will and Testament

I, Jane Doe-Mark of 50 Richmond Park, London OL4 2WX, being of sound mind, make this Will as my Last Will and Testament.

I hereby revoke all former Wills, Codicils, or other Testamentary instruments made by me. This Will relates to all my assets located in England and Wales.

1. I appoint my husband Edward Mark of 50 Richmond Park, London OL4 2WX as sole Executor of this my Will.

2. In the event that he should predecease me or be unwilling or unable to act, I appoint the following persons as Executors and Trustees of my Will: my sister Annie Doe-Blackwell of 40 Sunset Boulevard, London SW1 5RJ; my cousin Lacy Brown of 50 Acre Close, London, SW5 4XZ, and my brother-in-law Paul Mark of 70 Skyline Close, London SW1 2LJ.

3. In this Will, the term Trustees shall mean those of my Executors who obtain probate of this Will and Trustees of any Trust arising under this Will.

4. My Trustees shall hold the residue of my estate upon Trust for Sale with the power to postpone the sale and to accumulate the income of any of my children under the age of 25 and have the power at their own discretion to apply the income to the needs of that

child or those children and to cater for their maintenance, education, or needs.

5. The standard provisions and all the special provisions of the Society of Trust and Estate Practitioners (2ⁿᵈ Edition) shall apply.

6. Section 31 of the Trustee Act 1925 is hereby excluded and shall not apply to any Trust arising under this Will.

7. I direct that all my just debts and funeral expenses be paid as soon as reasonably practicable after my death.

8. I give all of my property to my husband Edward Mark absolutely, should he survive me by 30 days. In the event that we should both pass in the same incident, the residue of my estate shall be held by my Trustees for the benefit of my children equally, per stirpes, until they have attained the age of 25 years.

9. For the avoidance of doubt, in the event that any of my children have predeceased me leaving issue, I give to any of their children equally (my grandchildren) who survive me the share which would have fallen to that child upon attaining the age of 25 years.

10. Should I survive my husband and become the sole surviving parent while my children are still minors, I appoint my sister Annie Doe-Blackwell of 40 Sunset Boulevard, London SW1 5RJ, as Guardian of any of

my children under the age of 18. However, should she be unwilling or unable to act, I appoint my brother-in-law, Paul Mark of 70 Skyline Close, London SW1 2LJ, as their legal Guardian.

11. In the unlikely event that my husband, children, and I should all pass in the same event, with my children leaving no issue, I direct that all of my estate be divided equally between the children of my sister Annie Doe-Blackwell of 40 Sunset Boulevard, London SW1 5RJ, namely Jake and John Blackwell, and my brother-in-law Paul Mark of 70 Skyline Close, London SW1 2LJ.

12. Should any of the beneficiaries in clause 9 of this Will predecease me, leaving no issue, I give to the surviving beneficiaries, equally, the portion which would have fallen to that Beneficiary.

13. I wish to be cremated.

14. Should my cat Felix survive me, I wish for him to be cared for by my nephew Jake Blackwell of 40 Sunset Boulevard, London SW1 5RJ.

15. I give the residue of my estate to the registered charity "Cats' Lives Matter," Charity Number #20192020, whose registered address is 148 Hatton Cross, London SW1 2HL.

As witness my hand this [*date*] day of [*month*] 202[…]
[*signature of Jane Doe-Mark*]

Signed by the Testator in our presence and attested by us, as witnesses, in the presence of the Testator and of each other.

Witness 1:
Name:
Occupation:
Address:
Signature:

Witness 2:
Name:
Occupation:
Address:
Signature:

Mirror Will of Edward Mark:

Last Will and Testament

I, Edward Mark of 50 Richmond Park, London OL4 2WX, being of sound mind, make this Will as my Last Will and Testament.

I hereby revoke all former Wills, Codicils, or other Testamentary instruments made by me. This Will relates to all my assets located in England and Wales.

1. I appoint my wife Jane Doe-Mark of 50 Richmond Park, London OL4 2WX as sole Executrix of this my Will.

2. In the event that she should predecease me or be unwilling or unable to act, I appoint the following persons as Executors and Trustees of my Will: my sister-in-law Annie Doe-Blackwell of 40 Sunset Boulevard, London SW1 5RJ; my wife's cousin Lacy Brown of 50 Acre Close, London SW5 4XZ; and my brother Paul Mark of 70 Skyline Close, London SW1 2LJ.

3. In this Will, the term Trustees shall mean those of my Executors who obtain probate of this Will and Trustees of any Trust arising under this Will.

4. My Trustees shall hold the residue of my estate upon Trust for Sale with the power to postpone the sale

and to accumulate the income of any of my children under the age of twenty-five and have the power at their own discretion to apply income and capital to the needs of that child or those children and to cater for their maintenance, education, or benefit.

5. The standard provisions and all the special provisions of the Society of Trust and Estate Practitioners (2nd Edition) shall apply.

6. Section 31 of the Trustee Act 1925[9] is hereby excluded and shall not apply to any Trust arising under this Will.

7. I direct that all my just debts and funeral expenses be paid as soon as reasonably practicable after my death.

8. I give all of my property to my wife Jane Doe- Mark absolutely, should she survive me by 30 days. In the event that we should both pass in the same incident, the residue of my estate shall be held by my Trustees for the equal benefit of my children, per stirpes, until they have attained the age of twenty-five years.

9. For the avoidance of doubt, in the event that any of my children have predeceased me leaving issue, I give to any of their children equally (my grandchildren) who survive me the share which would have fallen to that child upon attaining the age of 25 years.

———————————————

10. Should I survive my wife and become the sole surviving parent while my children are still minors, I appoint my sister-in-law Annie Doe-Blackwell of 40 Sunset Boulevard, London SW1 5RJ as Guardian of any of my children under the age of 18. However, should she be unwilling or unable to act, I appoint my brother Paul Mark of 70 Skyline Close, London SW1 2LJ, as their legal Guardian.

11. In the unlikely event that my wife, children, and I should all pass in the same event, with my children leaving no issue, I direct that all of my estate be divided equally between the children of my sister-in-law Annie Doe-Blackwell of 40 Sunset Boulevard, London SW1 5RJ, namely Jake and John Blackwell, and my brother Paul Mark of 70 Skyline Close, London SW1 2LJ.

12. Should any of the beneficiaries in clause 9 of this Will predecease me, leaving no issue, I give the remaining beneficiaries equally the portion which would have fallen to that beneficiary.

13. I wish to be cremated.

14. Should my cat Felix survive me, I wish for him to be cared for by my nephew Jake Blackwell of 40 Sunset Boulevard, London SW1 5RJ.

15. I give the residue of my estate to the registered charity "Cats' Lives Matter," Charity Number

#20192020, whose registered address is 148 Hatton Cross, London SW1 2HL.

As witness my hand this [*date*] day of [*month*] 202[…]

[*signature of Edward Mark*]

Signed by the Testator in our presence and attested by us, as witnesses, in the presence of the Testator and of each other.

Witness 1:
Name:
Occupation:
Address:
Signature:

Witness 2:
Name:
Occupation:
Address:
Signature:

THINGS TO CONSIDER

Set up Trust for the kids as early as possible. A Trust Fund is as simple as a bank account at your local bank, with the name of the child on it and your name as the Trustee. It really is not rocket science. Place all cash gift sums in there and use it as a dumping ground to save for them.

This cash will be considered their cash, not yours, and this Trust will incur no charges while the children are between nought and eighteen years old. Between eighteen and twenty-five years old, the charge is a minimal 4.2%, much smaller than 40% inheritance tax.

CHAPTER 13

SETTING UP TRUST

Jane was delighted that they had finally got their Wills in place to make provision for the children should anything happen to her or Edward. She was still worried about the children inheriting their Pension pots, Death in Service, and Life Insurance at eighteen, as those sums were likely to be large.

Jane had left her employment to look after the children, and her Death in Service was no longer active as she had left her employment with the supermarket. She still had her Pension pot and Life Insurance. Edward still enjoyed all three benefits. They had informed the Solicitor that they would decide upon the nomination of those benefits. They agreed that they wanted the children to benefit, but their only concern should they not be around when the children turned eighteen was that the children would have access to large sums of money without the necessary and good sense to manage their finances.

They had learnt from the Solicitor that there were different types of Trust Funds that they could set up for the benefit of the children.

One such Trust was a bare Trust which they could use to accumulate birthday gifts and other resources for the children as they grew up. The fund would be seen as belonging to the children, with them as the parents managing the fund until the children were eighteen years old.

The Solicitor had explained that they could use such a Trust to make use of their annual allowances and potentially exempt transfers to save funds for the children till their eighteenth birthdays, thereby ensuring that they had some funds but not the entire estate at age eighteen, should they pass before the eighteenth birthdays of the children.

He explained that different types of Trusts were governed by different rules, some having fees[10][10] charged on items entering the Trust at 20%, items exiting at 4.2%, and the ten-year anniversary charge.

They wanted to decide which of these Trusts they might use and how best to protect the interests of the children by using Trust. Jane and Edward went over the main types of Trust again. They had been:

- Bare Trust – such as savings account for the children.
- Bereaved Minors Trust – a creation of statute, should they pass before the eighteenth birthdays of the children.
- Disabled Trust – to make provision for a disabled child.

- 18–25 Trust – to allow the children to inherit at an age above eighteen but not older than twenty-five.
- Relevant Property Trust – where the funds would be treated as belonging to the Trust, not the children. Usually used to make generational provisions for wealthy families and administered as a Discretionary Trust, giving the children no claim on the Trust Property but allowing them to be benefited at the discretion of the Trustees.
- Discretionary Trust – Trustees decide who to benefit.
- Immediate Post Death Interest – where someone gains an interest in something, such as a life interest, as soon as the Testator or person who made the Will dies.
- Charitable Trust – to benefit a cause.

Of all these Trusts, they wanted to consider the Bare Trust for the children and the Relevant Property Trust, where the assets in the Trust would be treated as not forming part of their estate. If the sums of money in the Life Insurance, Pension pots, and Death in Service were large, they could set up such a Trust and nominate it to receive those sums. The sums would be used for the benefit of the children by the Trustees, and they would not have to worry about the age of the children. Thus, protecting them and their generations going forward.

They considered the amounts of money they could put into their chosen Trust and whether they would want their children to become entitled at the age of eighteen years.

Considering the nil rate band, each of them could place £325,000 aside for the children giving them a total of £650,000, and once they survive seven years, these funds would no longer fall into their estate but would become exempt from inheritance tax.

Jane and Edward also considered using their annual allowance of £3,000 each. As they only had two children, they could give each child £3,000 each year into their account; this would be an exempt transfer for inheritance tax purposes.

If they were to do this every year till the children were eighteen, they could save a considerable sum for them, as much as £700,000 to £800,000 or more for each child having not taken into account small gifts from family and friends. Neither had they taken into account the Pension pot, the Death in Service, or the Life Insurance, which the children would benefit from should they pass before the children were eighteen years old.

They wanted to know what would happen should they pass within seven years of transferring into the Trust the nil rate band of £325,000 into the Trust. Or passing within seven years of making any gift into the Trust in excess of their nil rate band. This would give them a better understanding of the possible outcomes.

It was explained as follows:

Years	IHT Due
Less than 3	40%
More than 3 less than 4	32%
More than 4 less than 5	24%
More than 5 less than 6	16%
More than 7 less than 7	8%
7 years +	0%

Suppose they decided upon a Relevant Property Trust. In that case, they could put all or some of their assets in there to be managed as a discretionary trust, with the children as the beneficiaries. The children would have no entitlement to the Trust Funds. Jane and Edward would continue to exercise the role of Trustees and apply funds to the children as and when they saw fit, as the children grew. This would protect the children from creditors, bad marriages, gambling habits, or gold diggers.

Jane could see that their life was taking off nicely and believed that such a Trust should be given due consideration. If she and Edward were to pass, the funds would not be in their estate as it would be treated as a "Relevant Property Trust," with the assets being held on Discretionary Trust for the children. They had the option of setting up such a Trust in their lifetime to take advantage of the tax benefits and security of assets it would afford them.

In the end, Jane and Edward decided to set up separate Bare Trust Funds for each of their children which they could give them at eighteen. They considered that as Jane was no longer in employment, they really did not have the funds to gift the children their nil rate band every seven years. Further, Jane was no longer entitled to Death in Service, and her pension pot was small as she had left her employment.

They decided they were happy with the Will they had drafted with the Solicitor and wanted to wait and see how things would progress for them before deciding upon the need to set up a Relevant Property Trust. They were satisfied that under their Wills, the children would only benefit at the age of twenty-five if anything was to happen to them. However, the children would be entitled to any funds saved up for them over the years at the age of eighteen as those funds were being saved up as a bare trust.

Under their Wills, they had excluded the provisions of section 31 of the Trust Act 1925, entitling the children to income and capital at the age of eighteen and replaced the provision with a beneficial entitlement at the age of twenty-five, when they hoped the children would be more mature and sensible about money.

They had considered the powers of the Trustees and felt satisfied that they had chosen the right people to carry out this role. Jane noted with relief that all this would only come into effect after their passing if they were to pass before the children were twenty-five years old. She reminded Edward that they could write a letter of wishes to guide their Trustees on how to apply the funds to address the needs of the children if they should pass before the children were twenty-five years old.

The two of them sat down to consider what they would tell the Trustees about how the needs of their children should be met. They wanted to document their wishes. In any event, it could serve as a great reminder for them of their vision for the children. (Their draft letter of wishes is available in Appendix III.)

THINGS TO CONSIDER

If you are interested in setting up Trust for your children, consider carefully the type of Trust which would give you the greatest tax saving. It all depends on your net worth. Take into account how the entry, exit, and ten-year charges are calculated and how they may benefit you as opposed to paying 40% inheritance tax. Speak with a financial expert if necessary.

CHAPTER 14

PASSING ON THE BUSINESS

As the children grew, Edward longed to spend more time with them. Edward decided to set up his own engineering company. He knew that in time he would be able to fulfil his goal. He visited his Solicitors to set up the "Edward Mark Engineering Consultants" company. Jane had given up her job at the supermarket and was now a full-time mum.

The Solicitor had informed him that he could pass on the business tax-free[11][11] to his children should it qualify for business property relief. His business could qualify for this relief during his lifetime or on transfer at death by Will. His business did not have to be a company; it could also be a partnership or sole trader business. The relief can be claimed at 50% or 100% and can be claimed on property and buildings, unlisted shares, or machinery. The control of the business must be a controlling interest, and the business is valued at market value.[12][12]

Similar provisions apply to the passing on of agricultural property, such as land, pasture, woodland, and any building or machinery used in the day-to-day running of the farm.[13][13] The agricultural value[14][14] is used to calculate this relief. The agricultural property must have been used as a farm for at least two years before its transfer.

The passing on of businesses is a real game changer between the haves and the have-nots. The value which can be passed on is limitless once the business meets the qualifying criteria. Edward understood that he could pass millions, billions, or even trillions to his loved ones tax- free. This would surely render his Will tax efficient.

The Solicitor explained to him that the business had to meet these three conditions:

1. To be a business that would qualify for this relief, the business must have been established with a view to making profit. It must not consist wholly or mainly of investment holdings, dealings in securities, stocks or shares, or land and building holdings. This requires an expert's advice, as the company must be mainly providing a service and not mainly holding assets.
2. All the assets in the business had to be relevant business property. The terms "company" or "business" property really ring true here, as the assets in the business must be used as part of the operation of that business.
3. Length of ownership. The business must have been owned by the person who transferred it for at least two years before the transfer.

If he was to transfer the business during his lifetime, he would have to survive seven years. The person to whom he had transferred the business would need to keep it functioning as a business, ensuring that it qualified for the relief.

This made Edward think of how he could benefit even his great-grandchildren tax-free. He would have to speak with the Solicitor again if he wanted to go down this route to clarify the requirements, but for now, he would live in the hope that the law would not change anytime soon.

Edward thought long and hard about what this could mean. He knew he could pass on up to £1,000,000 worth of assets to his two children tax-free based on his joint nil rate band and residential nil rate band with Jane. Now, he could pass on so much more tax-free by taking advantage of business property relief. This was his opportunity to outwit the taxman.

THINGS TO CONSIDER

If your business qualifies for business property relief, be sure to secure that relief by passing the business on in your lifetime or in your Will. This is how some of the biggest inheritance tax savings are made, allowing you to benefit the next generation tax-free.

CHAPTER 15

IT'S COMPLICATED

Sometimes, life gets complicated. These complications arise because of changes in our circumstances. There is always a solution. Our feeling that the situation has become complicated arises from us not having formulated a strategy as to how best to tackle these changes. Having already discussed some aspects of divorce, let us look at some more of life's complications that may require changes to your Will.

Merged families

Merged families are on the rise due to reasons such as separation, divorce, and death of a loved one. Let's look at the example of a divorced person with children who has remarried to a partner with children or without children. If your circumstances are similar, it is best to start by speaking with a Will Writing Practitioner.

Here are a few things you should consider to protect the interest of your children. Remember that if you are divorced, any gift to your previous partner or any appointment of your previous partner as Executor, Trustee, etc., in your Will, will fail unless you express a contrary intention.[15][15]

Focus on arriving at a win-win position for all concerned. This may mean giving your new partner a life interest in the family home and then passing it on to your children from a previous relationship or giving an interest to your new spouse for a few years to allow them time to grieve and move on before passing the property on to your children or into Trust. Furthermore, it may mean making provision for the children during your lifetime, leaving you and your new partner free to make the most of your time together and be beholden to none.

The family home is always an issue and can become a bone of contention based on whose home it was before the two families merged. Communication is key in resolving any issue, and this matter is no different. It is also important to consider the children's age and maturity, whether the property is held as joint tenants or tenants in common, and whether or not any other transferrable nil rate bands are available to either party.

You may wish to consider placing the assets into a discretionary Relevant Property Trust, with clear guidelines on how the Trustees should provide for the children, if there are concerns surrounding life interest and whether the children are direct descendants or not, able to benefit from the residential nil rate band. A direct descendant includes[16][16] stepchildren, adopted children, or foster children of the deceased and their lineal descendants. Considering all these factors will help you determine the best strategy to apply.

Disabled Beneficiaries

In life, it is important to make provisions for less able people. This may mean less able to make decisions, physically or socially. To understand these provisions, we need to understand the definition of disabled[17][17] and have a beneficiary may qualify officially within the provisions of that legislation. Once that certification has been obtained, parliament has made it possible for those less able to benefit from Trusts[18][18] which can be established to look after their interest.

Winning the lottery

Many people believe that winning the lottery is not a complicated affair and that such a win would make their lives easier. Sometimes it does, but sometimes it is the beginning of challenges. The entire win immediately forms part of your estate, and if the win brings the value of your estate above £2,000,000, you will start losing entitlements such as your residential nil rate band.

At death, your estate will be subject to a 40% inheritance tax bill unless you have passed it all on to your spouse tax-free, or gifted it during your lifetime, seven years before death.

Gifts made within years of your death may be exempt if made to charities or other exempt bodies. Where the gifts made were potentially exempt and would only become exempt should you survive seven years, it is advisable to make the gift subject to the receiver paying inheritance tax thereon should you die within seven years of the gift being made. This way, your estate will be free from the burden of the inheritance tax, which may arise due to the gift.

Grossing up

"Grossing up" is a term mainly known to the accounting world and not usually considered by persons making a Will. It is important to limit the inheritance tax paid to a minimum. It is applied where the Testator agrees to pay the inheritance tax on any gift given to a Beneficiary. The value of the inheritance tax paid by the Testator is added back onto the gift and then taxed at 40%.

Consideration needs to be given to whether the Beneficiary should pay any inheritance tax arising on a gift to reduce the inheritance tax liability. The key to avoiding this provision is to ask yourself, "Is this gift being assigned to an exempt beneficiary such as a spouse or a charity?" If it is not, consider making the gift subject to the Beneficiary paying the tax arising thereon. Count the cost.

THINGS TO CONSIDER

If it's complicated, call in the experts.

CHAPTER 16

DEALING WITH MULTIPLE JURISDICTIONS

Foreign spouses

British law makes life a little complicated if your spouse is foreign and not domiciled in England and Wales. The idea of an unlimited transfer of assets between spouses at 0% inheritance tax will not apply to your foreign spouse. Your foreign spouse will only enjoy the benefit of a nil rate band of £325,000 when it comes to transfers between spouses.

The taxman moves the domicile goalpost as and when he desires to obtain his 40% inheritance tax objective. This is why you need to seek advice from someone who clearly understands what domicile or none domicile means to enable you to use this concept to your advantage.

There is also the option to "opt in," which means requesting that you would like to opt into the inheritance tax regime in England and Wales and be considered as domicile in England and Wales. There is also the option to "opt out," but each of these comes with its own advantages and disadvantages, which should be discussed and considered before writing your tax-efficient Will.

The word "domicile" frightens most seasoned Will Writers. It means your place of permanent residence or the place where you intend to reside permanently. As the law of England and Wales is known for its complications, the word can have several meanings.

Your domicile may be a domicile of origin. This usually means the place where you were born. You may be asked about your domicile of choice, which is the place you have decided to call home and where you actually live.

If you are a child or a spouse, you may have acquired a domicile of dependence based on where you have settled with your spouse or if you are a child where you may have settled with your parents.

English law also embraces the concept of habitual residence – some of us have homes around the world, and the taxman and the courts sometimes need to look at where we habitually reside to determine our domicile.

Domicile in the United Kingdom is deemed to have been acquired when you have been permanently resident in the United Kingdom for at least seventeen tax years out of the last twenty and is considered lost when you have not been here for at least four years.

Here in the UK, we have an excellent example of Meghan, a foreign spouse within the royal household. I am assuming here that royals pay tax, and reference to her case is for illustration only of the rules of domicile. Had she spent seventeen years here in the UK out of 20 tax years, she would have been deemed UK domicile and benefited from 0% transfers between spouses had her husband, Prince Harry, passed. Instead, they chose to leave Britain and move to the USA, where they decided to reside. After four tax years of Prince Harry living outside the UK, he would lose his UK domicile. During those four years before losing his UK domicile, had he passed, Meghan would only be entitled to a maximum benefit tax- free of £325,000. She is no better off now that the family has left the UK, as they will now be subjected to the US tax regime, which is not within the focus of this book.

THINGS TO CONSIDER

Have you considered the tax efficiency of your relationship?

CHAPTER 17

HOLOGRAPH WILLS

On occasion, you may be going on a journey that causes you concern, and you may not have time to speak with your Solicitor or your Will Writing Practitioner about your Will. In such circumstances, there is no need to panic. The law recognises Wills written in your own handwriting and signed and dated by you. Such Wills do not require witnesses.

For a Will to be valid, the requirements for making a valid Will still need to be achieved. Your Will must be made of your own free will and not under duress or undue influence. You must intend to distribute your estate and understand the consequences of your actions.

Such Wills are ideal for people in unsavoury circumstances such as on a battlefield, in an accident, at sea, realising their imminent demise or death.

The drawback of using this form of Will is that there may be no witnesses, and your handwriting may need to be proven if there is any doubt that you made the Will. However, should none of these concerns apply, you would certainly have a valid Will. Here is an example:

Last Will and Testament

I, James Brown, write this Will as my Last Will and Testament.

I revoke all previous Wills.

I appoint my son, Eric Brown, Executor of this my Will.

I request that all my just debts and funeral expenses be paid from my estate.

I give all my estate to my beloved son Eric Brown. Signed: James Brown

Dated: 31/12/2020

Such Wills have been known to contain even fewer words. One of the shortest-ever known Wills only states, "To my wife." There was no doubt that the Testator had made this Will as he was dying. The writing was his, and his actions had created a valid Will, which he intended to create at the time.

It is best, however, to discuss your circumstances with a professional who can guide you and advise you on how an inheritance tax liability could be minimised. That is the objective of this book, hence the title *How to Write a Tax-Efficient Will*. I do hope that you have benefited greatly from the suggested considerations and will now be taking steps towards writing your own tax-efficient Will.

THINGS TO CONSIDER

During an emergency, don't panic.
Consider a Holograph Will.

CHAPTER 18

THE WILL WRITING CHALLENGE

Here is an opportunity to put into practice what you have learnt in this book. Remember that you can write your own Will, but take time to consider the tax efficiency of your writing. If your circumstances are too complicated, contact the Author or your Trust and Estates Solicitor.

Here is a guide to help you structure the paragraphs of your Will. Let's get started:

1. Who are you? Provide your name and address.
2. What are you creating? Last Will and Testament.
3. Revocation of previous Wills clause.
4. Appointment of Executors and Trustees.
5. I appoint, as my Trustees, those of my Executors who obtain probate of this my Will.
6. "The standard provisions of the Society of Trust and Estate Practitioners (2nd Edition) shall apply. [This wording will incorporate the basic terms or powers of Trustees into your Will.]
7. Request that debts and funeral expenses be paid as soon as possible after your death.
8. Appointment of a Guardian if you have minor children.
9. The residue of my estate shall be held upon Trust for Sales with the power to postpone the sale.

10. "I give my" son of [address] per stirpes, my [house, car, etc.] upon attaining the age of 25 years.

11. The provisions of section 31 of the Trustee Act 1925 shall not apply to this Will. [If you would like your children to inherit after the age of eighteen, exclude section 31 of the Trustee Act 1925.]

12. Make provision for your pet.

13. Residue - if all your gifts fail or the persons you have nominated to receive gifts die before you, as a last resort, who or what would you like to benefit?

14. Attestation - this clause lets the world know that you are confirming the creation of your Will by your signature. "As Witness my hand this [--] day of [--] 20[--]

15. Witnessing - ensure that you sign in the presence of your two witnesses and that they sign in your presence, give their occupation and address after the following clause has been included:

"Signed by the Testator and attested by us, as witnesses, in the presence of the Testator and of each other."

Take the challenge by completing the practice example which   follows:

Last Will and Testament of

[Insert your name]

_____

I, [Your name]

_____

Of

_____

Postcode_____, being of sound mind, make this Will as my Last Will and Testament.

I revoke all previous Wills and Codicils made by me.

This Will relates to all my estate located in

_____

I appoint my [wife, husband, children, brother, sister, family friend, the partner in the firm of Solicitors X]

[name of person appointed]

_____

Of

_____

Postcode_____

And my [friend, sister, brother, neighbour][name of person]

_____

Of

_____

Postcode_____

as Executors and Trustees of this my Will.

I direct that all my debts and funeral expenses be paid as soon as possible after my death.

I appoint as Guardian of my minor children, my [friend, sister, brother, cousin] [name of person appointed]

_____

Of

_____

Postcode_____

I give, devise, and bequeath to my [friend, son, daughter etc]

_____

Of

_____

*Postcode*_____

[state item bequeathed or given]

———————————

I give to my[cousin, friend, political party, etc]

———————————

Of

———————————

*Postcode*_____

———————————

[state item given]

———————————

I wish to be [cremated, buried, donated to medical research]

———————————

[Provision for pets] I give my [dog, cat, snake, parrot] to

———————————

Of

———————————

The residue of my estate I give to

_____

_____

As witness my hand this [*date*] day of [*month*] 202[…]

[_____]

Signed by the Testator and attested by us, as witnesses, in the presence of the Testator and of each other.

Witness 1:	
Name:	
Occupation:	
Address:	
Signature:	
Email:	

Witness 2:	
Name:	
Occupation:	
Address:	
Signature:	
Email:	

We have come to the end of this work, but I hope you have found it informative and useful. You will find the information provided in the Appendices below useful. Follow me on Facebook @ Tax Efficient Wills UK or come join the group.

SUBSCRIBE to my YouTube Channel, where I have provided lots of free information videos on: Deborah Bowers   Channel: https://www.youtube.com/channel/UCgJHrKI6u7CocwKS_3 KUkVw

Take the How to Write a Tax Efficient Will Course, where I take you step by step through the inheritance tax provisions, showing you how you can saving it, and allow your beneficiaries to enjoy the assets you have left them, rather than having to sell the assets to pay inheritance tax. By the end of the course you will be able to write your own tax efficient will or you can book a 1-2-1 to take a deep dive into your personal circumstances.

Contact me at: Deborahbowerswillwriting@gmail.comOr via my website: https://deborahbowerswillwritingservices.com/

APPENDIX I:

ASSETS AND LIABILITIES

Assets	Description	Value
Residential Property		
Other Properties		
Cash and Deposit Accounts		
Account (1)		
Account (2)		
Account (3)		
Account (4)		
Stocks and Shares		
Company (1)		
Company (2)		
Company (3)		
Vehicles		
Vehicle (1)		
Vehicle (2)		
Vehicle (3)		

Valuables		
Art		
Jewellery		
Antiques		
Businesses		
Internet Business		
YouTube Channels		
Royalties		
Other Assets		
Bitcoin		
TOTAL ASSETS		£
LIABILITIES	**Description**	**Value**
Residential Mortgage		
Mortgage on Other Property		
Mortgage on Business Property		
Other Mortgages		
Loans	**Description**	**Balanc**

		e
Car Loan (Hire Purchase)		
Car Loan (Hire Purchase)		
Car Loan (Hire Purchase)		
Credit Cards		
Card (1)		
Card (2)		
Card (3)		
Card (4)		
Overdraft (1)		
Overdraft (2)		
Overdraft (3)		
Other Debts (1)		
Other Debts (2)		
Debts to Family and Friends		
Other		
TOTAL LIABILITIES		£
NET ASSETS (Assets Less Liabilities)		£
ASSETS TO PASSING OUTSIDE	Description/Nominat	Value

136

ESTATE	ion	
Pension (1)		
Pension (2)		
Life Insurance (1)		
Life Insurance (2)		
Death in Service Benefit		

PERSONAL CONSIDERATIONS

Getting Prepared

PERSONAL DETAILS

Name, middle names, surname:

_____

_____

Former names:

_____

_____

Confirmation of age (18+) will do:

_____

Occupation:

_____

Address:

_____

_____

Telephone number:

Email: _____

Marital status: _____

Country of Birth: _____

Country of permanent residence: _____

Type of Will required:

Mirror Will_____

Mutual Will_____

Single Will_____

DETAILS OF SPOUSE

Name, middle names, surname: _____

Former names: _____

Confirmation of age (D.O.B.): _____

Occupation:

_____

Address:

_____

_____

Postcode:

_____

Telephone number:

_____

Email:

_____

Length of time of residence in UK to date:

_____

Country of Birth:

_____

SCOPE OF WILL

Please tick as appropriate.

Is this Will to be:

a) A worldwide Will

_____

b) Relate to property only in England and Wales

_____

c) Exclude property in any county?

_____

CHILDREN

Full names including middle names. Age or D.O.B.:

1 _____

2 _____

3 _____

4 _____

LOCATION OF ASSETS, TYPE OF ASSET

1. _____

2. _____

EXECUTORS (18+)

Name, middle names, surname:

_____

_____

Full address, email, telephone number, and relationship to you.

Address:

_____

_____

Email:

_____

Telephone number:

_____

Relationship to you:

_____

Full address, email, telephone number, and relationship to you.

Address:

_____

_____

Email:

_____

Telephone number:

_____

Relationship to you:

_____

Full address, email, telephone number, and relationship to you.

Address:

_____

_____

Email:

_____

Telephone number:

_____

Relationship to you:

_____

EXECUTORS

_____

_____

Full address, email, telephone number, and relationship to you.

Address:

_____

_____

Email:

Telephone number: _____

Relationship to you: _____

Indicate which persons should act together or order of preference of appointment.

_____

_____

TRUSTEES (18+)

(Please note that your Executors can also act as your Trustees.)

Address and relationship to you:

1. Full name: _____

Address: _____

_____

Email: _____

Telephone number:

_____

Relationship to you:

_____

2. Full name:

_____

Address:

_____

_____

Email:

_____

Telephone number:

_____

Relationship to you:

_____

3. Full name:

_____

Address:

_____

_____

Email:

_____

Telephone number:

_____

Relationship to you:

_____

4. Full name:

_____

Address:

_____

_____

Email:

_____

Telephone number:

_____

Relationship to you:

_____

TRUSTEES CONTINUED

Indicate which persons should act together or order of preference of appointment.

_____

_____

GUARDIANS (18+)

Who would you like to appoint as Guardians?

Full Name:

_____

Full Address:

_____

_____

Postcode:

_____

Relationship to you:

_____

Age of Guardian:

_____

SPOUSE EXECUTOR/TRUSTEE/BENEFICIARY

Would you like to appoint your spouse as sole Executor and Trustee should your spouse predecease you?

Yes:

No:

Should you and your spouse pass in the same incident, would you like to appoint the children who have attained the age of majority?

Yes:

No:

Indicate the preferred age at which children should act as Executors and Trustees:

_____

_____

At what age would you like the children to inherit?

_____

Would you like any gift to your child(ren) to go to any child(ren) they leave behind?

Yes:

No:

At what age would you like the grandchildren to inherit?

_____

OTHER BENEFICIARIES

1. Full name, including middle names:

_____

Address:

_____

_____

Postcode:

_____

Relationship to you:

_____

2. Full name, including middle names:

_____

Address:

_____

_____

Postcode:

_____

Relationship to you:

_____

TRUST

Please tick as appropriate.

Would you like to set up a Will Trust (a Trust which comes into effect at death)?

Yes:

No:

Who are the intended Beneficiaries under the Trust?

_____

Who would you like to appoint as the Trustees of this Trust?

Full name and address:

_____

_____

What type of Trust is it to be? Please circle.

Bare Trust

Bereaved Minors Trust

Disabled Trust

Discretionary Trust

Charitable Trust

Interest in Possession Trust

18–25 Trust

Other

Would you like to set up a Lasting Power of Attorney[19][19] (a Lasting Power of Attorney enables you to appoint persons to administer your own affairs if you are deemed unable to do so by a medical practitioner)?

_____

Yes:

No:

Who would you like to appoint as Trustees?

1. Full name, including middle names:

_____

Address:

_____

_____

Postcode:

_____

Relationship to you:

_____

Full name, including middle names:

_____

Address:

_____

_____

Postcode:

_____

Relationship to you:

_____

What powers would you like your Trustees to have?

_____

_____

RESIDUE:

Who would you like to give the residue of your estate?

_____

_____

PETS

Name of pet:

_____

Type of pet:

_____

Who would you like to have your pet should it survive you?

Full name:

_____

Address:

_____

_____

Post code:

_____

Relationship to you:

_____

BURIED OR CREMATED

Would you like to be:

Buried?

Cremated?

Donated for medical research:

All of you:

Which parts:

_____

Specify any parts you would like to keep:

_____

Have you made your request known to any medical institution?

Yes:

No:

Has your request been accepted?

Yes:

No:

Other Instructions:

APPENDIX III:

LETTER OF WISHES

This is a letter you write to your Trustees, Guardians, or even Beneficiaries to tell them what you would love them to do. It is not enforceable, but it enables them to know your expectations. For example, you may wish to tell your Guardian where to educate the children, etc. Here is an example:

Dear Annie, you have been such a wonderful sister, friend, and a shoulder to lean on all these years. The children love and adore you, and you have always treated them as your own. It is my wish that they will grow up to be adults who will make both of us proud.

You know that Lisa tends to be a bit more fragile, but I know she will come into her own someday. It is my hope that they shall both be sent off to St. George's Boarding School, where I know that they will be provided with the best of a British education. Eric has always spoken of becoming a physician, do encourage him along that path. I hope the Trust Fund will be big enough to fund his education and help him achieve his goal. Please resist the temptation to buy him a farer at eighteen. He loves his cars, but he will have to work to buy one with his own cash if it is up to me. Please do not give in to his pleas.

Lisa being the delicate flower that she is, has always enjoyed her ballet and would love to become a professional dancer. Please do your best to get her into the finest academy; this area of work is so very competitive, and only a few break-through financially. I know, however, that her love and passion for the arts will see her through.

Always   in   your   hearts.   XX

HOW YOUR ASSETS ARE DIVIDED IF YOU DIE INTESTATE (WITHOUT A WILL) IN ENGLAND AND WALES

HOW YOUR ASSETS ARE DIVIDED IF YOU DIE INTESTATE (WITHOUT A WILL) IN SCOTLAND

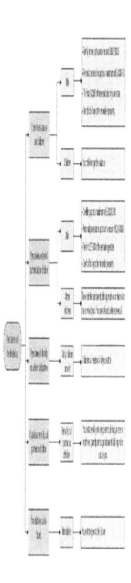

161

STEP STANDARD PROVISIONS2ND EDITION
(ENGLAND AND WALES)

The *STEP Standard Provisions* is a publication for practitioners who draft Wills subject to the law of England and Wales. It sets out clear provisions to include in a Will, avoiding technical terms that may confuse the lay reader.

Any properly drafted Will or Settlement must contain a large amount of text dealing with routine administrative matters. It had been necessary to set this out in full in each Will until STEP condensed this material into its Standard Provisions, which was first published in 1992 and is now in its second edition.

Trust law has changed considerably since the first edition, and the updated *STEP Standard Provisions* reflect this. The most significant amendment is that there is now a choice to incorporate either the "core" provisions or the fuller form when drafting a document. The second edition also attempts to address an issue that concerned the Drafters and consultees: the possible misuse of powers conferred by the Provisions.

The *STEP Standard Provisions* (second edition) was led and mainly drafted by James Kessler QC TEP. The accompanying guidance notes, which are provided for Will-drafting practitioners who know the first edition and want to know what has changed, were drafted by Toby Harris TEP. Society is grateful to James, Toby, and all the consultants for their hard work on behalf of the entire profession.

STEP applied for a Practice Direction from the Principal Registry of the Family Division, as was granted for the first edition, permitting Wills incorporating the *STEP Standard Provisions* (second edition) by reference to be proved in the normal way, without providing text of the Provisions themselves. This was granted on 30 January 2013, and the appropriate circular has now been issued to notify the Probate Service that the second edition has been lodged with, and accepted by, the Senior District Judge. There is no need to refer to the STEP Provisions in the oath nor to lodge a copy of them with the application to prove a Will that incorporates them. This Practice Direction does not supersede the earlier Direction, so there will be no effect on documents that incorporate the first edition.

Patricia Wass TEP, Chair, STEP England and Wales (2013)

PROVISIONS OF THE SOCIETY OF TRUST AND ESTATE PRACTITIONERS

The text of the second edition of the *STEP Standard Provisions* is as follows:

1 Incorporation of STEP Provisions

1.1 These Provisions (with the exception of the Special Provisions) may be incorporated in a document by the words:

The Standard Provisions of the Society of Trust and Estate Practitioners (2nd Edition) shall apply

or in any manner indicating an intention to incorporate them.

1.2 These Provisions (including all the Special Provisions) may be incorporated in a document by the words:

The Standard Provisions and all of the Special Provisions of the Society of Trust and Estate Practitioners (2nd Edition) shall apply

or in any manner indicating an intention to incorporate them.

1.3 These Provisions (including specified Special Provisions) may be incorporated in a document by the words:

The Standard Provisions and the following Special Provisions of the Society of Trust and Estate Practitioners (2nd Edition) shall apply:

[specify which Special Provisions apply, as appropriate]

or in any manner indicating an intention to incorporate them.

1.4 The Special Provisions shall not be incorporated in a document only by the words:

The Standard Provisions of the Society of Trust and Estate Practitioners (2ⁿᵈ Edition) shall apply

in the absence of the words "Special Provisions" or some other expression of an intention to incorporate them.

2 Interpretation

2.1 In these Provisions, unless the context otherwise requires:

2.1.1 **"Civil Partner"** has the same meaning as in section 1 of the Civil Partnership Act 2004.

2.1.2 **"Income Beneficiary,"** in relation to Trust Property, means a Person to whom income of the Trust Property is payable (as of right or at the discretion of the Trustees).

2.1.3 **"Person"** includes a Person anywhere in the world and includes a Trustee.

2.1.4 **"Principal Document"** means the document in which these Provisions are incorporated.

2.1.5 **"Special Provisions"** means the Provisions in clauses 14–23 of these Provisions.

2.1.6 **"Trust"** means any Trust created by the Principal Document and an estate of a deceased Person to which the Principal Document relates.

2.1.7 **"Trustees"** means the personal representatives or Trustees of the Trust for the time being.

2.1.8 **"Trust Fund"** means the property comprised in the Trust for the time being.

2.1.9 **"Trust Property"** means any property comprised in the Trust Fund.

2.2 These Provisions have effect subject to the Provisions of the Principal Document.

3 Protection for Interest in Possession Trusts

If the existence of any powers conferred by these Provisions would be enough (without their exercise) to prevent a Person from being entitled to an interest in possession (within the meaning of the Inheritance Tax Act 1984), then those powers shall be restricted so far as necessary to avoid that result.

4 Additional Powers

The Trustees shall have the following powers:

4.1 Investment
The Trustees may invest Trust Property in any manner as if they were absolutely entitled to it. In particular, the Trustees may invest in land in any part of the world and unsecured loans.

4.2 Management
The Trustees may affect any transaction relating to the management or disposition of Trust Property as if they were absolutely entitled to it.

In particular:

4.2.1 The Trustees may repair and maintain Trust Property.

4.2.2 The Trustees may develop or improve Trust Property.

4.3 Joint Property

The Trustees may acquire property jointly with any Person.

4.4 Income and Capital

Income may be set aside and invested to answer any liabilities which, in the opinion of the Trustees, ought to be borne out of income or to meet depreciation of the capital value of any Trust Property. In particular, income may be applied for a leasehold sinking fund policy.

4.5 Accumulated Income

The Trustees may apply accumulated income as if it were income arising in the current year.

4.6 Use of Trust Property

4.6.1 The Trustees may acquire any interest in property anywhere in the world for occupation or use by an Income Beneficiary.

4.6.2 The Trustees may permit an Income Beneficiary to occupy or use Trust Property on such terms as they think fit.

4.6.3 This clause does not restrict any right of Beneficiaries to occupy land under the Trusts of Land and Appointment of Trustees Act 1996.

4.7 Application of Trust Capital

4.1.1 The Trustees may:

(i) lend money which is Trust Property to an Income Beneficiary without security, on such terms as they think fit,

(ii) guarantee the debts or obligations of an Income Beneficiary,

(iii) charge Trust Property as security for debts or obligations of an Income Beneficiary, or

(iv) pay money which is Trust Property to an Income Beneficiary as his income for the purpose of augmenting his income.

4.7.2 Clause 4.7.1 applies only if:

(i) the Trustees have power to transfer that Trust Property to that Income Beneficiary absolutely, or

(ii) the Trustees have power to do so with the consent of another Person and the Trustees act with the written consent of that Person.

4.8 Trade

The Trustees may carry on a trade in any part of the world, alone or in partnership.

4.9 Deposit of Documents

The Trustees may deposit documents relating to the Trust (including bearer securities) with any Person.

4.10 Nominees

The Trustees may vest Trust Property in any Person as nominee, may authorise the use of sub-nominees, and may place Trust Property in the possession or control of any Person.

4.11 Place of Administration

The Trustees may carry on the administration of the Trust anywhere they think fit.

4.12 Payment of Tax

The Trustees may pay tax liabilities of the Trust (and interest on such tax) even though such liabilities are not enforceable against the Trustees.

4.13 Indemnities

The Trustees may indemnify any Person for any liability properly chargeable against Trust Property.

4.14 Security

The Trustees may charge Trust Property as security for any liability properly incurred by them as Trustees.

4.15 Appropriation

The Trustees may appropriate Trust Property to any Person or class of Persons in or towards the satisfaction of their interest in the Trust Fund.

4.16 Receipt by Charities, etc.

4.16.1 Where Trust Property is to be paid or transferred to a charity or non-charitable association or company, the receipt of the treasurer or appropriate officer of the organisation shall be a complete discharge to the Trustees. A Trustee shall not be liable for making a payment or transfer to any Person who appears to be the treasurer or appropriate officer unless, at the time of the distribution, the Trustee has knowledge of circumstances which call for enquiry.

4.16.2If any charity ceases to exist, changes its name, or enters into insolvent liquidation before the time that a gift to the charity takes effect in possession, the gift shall instead be paid to such charity as the Trustees decide having regard to the objects that were intended to benefit.

4.17 Release of Powers

The Trustees may by Deed release any of their powers wholly or in part so as to bind future Trustees.

4.18 Ancillary Powers

The Trustees may do anything which is incidental or conducive to the exercise of their functions.

5 Powers of Maintenance and Advancement

Sections 31 and 32 of the Trustee Act 1925 shall apply with the following modifications.

5.1 The proviso to section 31(1) shall be deleted.

5.2 The words "one half of" in section 32(1)(a) shall be deleted.

6 Minors and Beneficiaries Without Capacity: Powers Over Income

6.1 Where the Trustees may apply income for the benefit of a minor, they may do so by paying the income to the minor's parent or Guardian on behalf of the minor or to the minor if they have attained the age of 16. A Trustee is under no duty to enquire into the use of the income unless the Trustee has knowledge of circumstances which call for enquiry.

6.2 Where the Trustees may apply income for the benefit of a minor, they may do so by resolving that they hold that income on Trust for the minor absolutely and:

6.2.1 The Trustees may apply that income for the benefit of the minor during his minority.

6.2.2 The Trustees shall transfer the residue of that income to the minor on attaining the age of 18.

6.2.3 For investment and other administrative purposes, that income shall be treated as Trust Property.

6.3 Where income is payable to a Beneficiary who does not have the mental capacity to appoint an attorney under a Lasting Power of Attorney which relates to the property and affairs of the Beneficiary, the Trustees may (subject to the directions of the court or a deputy appointed under the Mental Capacity Act 2005 whose powers include receiving such income) apply that income for the benefit of the Beneficiary.

6.4 Where the Trustees may pay or apply income to or for the benefit of a Beneficiary who does not have the mental capacity to give a receipt, the Trustees may pay the income to the Person having or appearing to the Trustees to have the care and financial responsibility for such a Person. A Trustee is under no duty to enquire into the use of the income unless the Trustee has knowledge of circumstances which call for enquiry.

7 Disclaimer

A Person may disclaim his interest under the Trust wholly or in part.

8 Apportionment

Income and expenditure shall be treated as arising when payable, and not from day to day, so that no apportionment shall take place.

9 Conflicts of Interest

9.1 In this clause:

9.1.1 **"Fiduciary"** means a Person subject to Fiduciary duties under the Trust.

9.1.2 **"Independent Trustee,"** in relation to a Person, means a Trustee who is not:

(i) that Person;
(ii) a brother, sister, ancestor, descendant, or dependent of the Person;
(iii) a spouse or Civil Partner of (i) or (ii) above; or
(iv) a company controlled by one or more Persons within (i) (ii) or (iii) above.

9.2 A Fiduciary may:

9.2.1 enter into a transaction with the Trustees, or

9.2.2 be interested in an arrangement in which the Trustees are or might have been interested, or

9.2.3 act (or not act) in any other circumstances even though his Fiduciary duty under the Trust conflicts with other duties or with his personal interest.

9.3 Clause 9.2 has effect only in relation to administrative and not dispositive matters, and only applies if:

9.3.1 the Fiduciary first discloses to the Trustees the nature and extent of any material interest conflicting with his Fiduciary duties, and

9.3.2 there is in relation to the Fiduciary an Independent Trustee in respect of whom there is no conflict of interest, and he considers that the transaction arrangement or action is not contrary to the general interest of the Trust.

9.4 The powers of the Trustees may be used to benefit a Trustee (to the same extent as if he were not a Trustee) provided that:

9.4.1 there is in relation to that Trustee an Independent Trustee in respect of whom there is no conflict of interest or

9.4.2 the Trustees consist of or include all the Trustees originally appointed under the Principal Document.

10 Trustee Remunerations

10.1 A Trustee acting in a professional capacity is entitled to receive reasonable remuneration out of the Trust Fund for any services that he provides to or on behalf of the Trust.

10.2 For this purpose, a Trustee acts in a professional capacity if he acts in the course of a profession or business which consists of or includes the Provision of services in connection with:

10.2.1 the management or administration of Trusts generally or a particular kind of Trust, or

10.2.2 any particular aspect of the management or administration of Trusts generally or a particular kind of Trust.

10.3 The Trustees may make arrangements to remunerate themselves for work done for a company connected with the Trust Fund.

11 Trust Corporations

11.1 A Trust Corporation appointed by the Principal Document may act as Trustee on the basis of its standard terms as published at the date of the Principal Document.

11.2 On the appointment of a Trust Corporation as Trustee, the parties to the appointment may provide that the Trust Corporation may act as Trustee on the basis of its standard terms as published at the date of the appointment (in which case clause 11.1 shall not apply).

11.3 The Trust Corporation is entitled to receive remuneration and other charges in accordance with those terms.

11.4 In the event of a conflict between those terms and these Provisions, those terms shall prevail.

11.5 In this clause, "Trust Corporation" has the same meaning as in the Trustee Act 1925.

12 Liability of Trustees

12.1 A Trustee shall not be liable for a loss to the Trust Fund unless that loss was caused by his own actual fraud or negligence.

12.2 A Trustee shall not be liable for a loss to the Trust Fund unless that loss or damage was caused by his own actual fraud, provided that:

12.2.1 the Trustee acts as a lay Trustee (within the meaning of section 28 of the Trustee Act 2000); and

12.2.2 there is another Trustee who does not act as a lay Trustee.

12.3 A Trustee shall not be liable for acting in accordance with the advice of counsel, of at least five years standing, with respect to the Trust. The Trustees may, in particular, conduct legal proceedings in accordance with such advice without obtaining a court order. A Trustee may recover from the Trust Fund any expenses where he has acted in accordance with such advice.

12.4 Clause 12.3 does not apply:

12.4.1 in relation to a Trustee who knows or has reasonable cause to suspect that the advice was given in ignorance of material facts;

12.4.2 if proceedings are pending to obtain the decision of the court on the matter;

12.4.3 in relation to a Trustee who has a personal interest in the subject matter of the advice; or

12.4.6 in relation to a Trustee who has committed a breach of Trust relating to the subject matter of the advice.

12.5 Clause 12.3 does not prejudice any right of any Person to follow property or income into the hands of any Person, other than a purchaser, who may have received it.

13 Subsequent editions of *STEP standard provisions*

13.1 Subject to clauses 13.2 and 13.3 below, the Trustees may by Deed declare that any subsequent edition of the *Provisions* of the Society of Trust and Estate Practitioners shall apply in place of these *Provisions* wholly or in part.

13.2 If the Special Provisions are not all incorporated into the Principal Document, the Trustees do not have power under this clause to incorporate:

13.2.1 Special Provisions which are not incorporated into the Principal Document, or substantially similar powers or

13.2.2 any other Provisions described in the subsequent edition of the *Standard Provisions* as Special Provisions.

13.3 The new edition of the *Provisions* shall have effect subject to the Provisions of the Principal Document.

SPECIAL PROVISIONS

14 Borrowing

The Trustees may borrow money for investment or any other purpose. Money borrowed shall be treated as Trust Property.

15 Delegation

A Trustee may delegate in writing any of his functions to any Person. None of the restrictions on delegation in sections 12–15 of the Trustee Act 2000 shall apply. A Trustee shall not be responsible for the default of that Person (even if the delegation was not strictly necessary or expedient) provided that he took reasonable care in his selection and supervision.

16 Supervision of Company

A Trustee is under no duty to enquire into the conduct of a company in which the Trustees are interested unless the Trustee has knowledge of circumstances that call for an enquiry.

17 Powers of Maintenance: Deferring Income Entitlement to 21

17.1 For the purposes of section 31 of the Trustee Act 1925, a Person shall be treated as attaining the age of majority at the Specified Age, and the references to the age of eighteen years in section 31 shall be treated as references to the Specified Age.

17.2 In this clause, the "Specified Age" means the age of 21 or such earlier age (not being less than 18) as the Trustees may by Deed specify.

18 Minors and Beneficiaries Without Capacity: Powers Over Trust Capital

18.1 Where the Trustees may apply capital for the benefit of a minor, they may do so by paying the capital to the minor's parent or Guardian on behalf of the minor or to the minor if they have attained the age of 16. A Trustee is under no duty to enquire into the use of the capital unless the Trustee has knowledge of circumstances which call for enquiry.

18.2 Where capital is payable to a Beneficiary who does not have the mental capacity to appoint an attorney under a Lasting Power of Attorney which relates to the property and affairs of the Beneficiary, the Trustees may (subject to the directions of the court or a deputy appointed under the Mental Capacity Act whose powers include receiving such capital) apply that capital for the benefit of the Beneficiary.

18.3 Where the Trustees may pay or apply capital to or for the benefit of a Beneficiary who does not have the mental capacity to give a receipt, the Trustees may pay the same to the Person having or appearing to the Trustees to have the care and financial responsibility for such Person. A Trustee is under no duty to enquire into the use of the capital unless the Trustee has knowledge of circumstances which call for enquiry.

19 Absolute Discretion Clause

The Trustees are not under any duty to consult with any Beneficiaries or to give effect to the wishes of any Beneficiaries. The powers of the Trustees may be exercised:

19.1 at their absolute discretion; and

19.2 from time to time as occasion requires.

20 Appointment and Retirement of Trustees

20.1 A Person may be appointed Trustee of the Trust even though he has no connection with the United Kingdom.

20.2 A Trustee may be discharged even though there is neither a Trust Corporation nor two Persons to act as Trustees provided that there remains at least one Trustee.

21 Powers Relating to Income and Capital

21.1 The Trustees are under no duty to hold a balance between conflicting interests of Persons interested in Trust Property. In particular:

21.1.1 the Trustees may acquire:

(i) wasting assets and

(ii) assets which yield little or no income for investment or any other purpose.

21.1.2 the Trustees are under no duty to procure distributions from a company in which they are interested.

21.2 The Trustees may pay taxes and other expenses out of income, although they would otherwise be paid out of capital.

22 Power to Appropriate at Value at Time of Death

22.1 Where:

22.1.1 these Provisions are incorporated into a Will,

22.1.2 the Trustees have ascertained the value of Trust Property on the death of the Testator, and

22.1.3 the Property is appropriated under clause 4.15 within three years of that death, the Trustees may adopt that valuation so that the value for the purposes of the appropriation shall be the value at the date of the death (instead of the value at the date of the appropriation).

22.2 Where clause 22.1 applies to an appropriation, any other valuation which may be required for the purposes of the same exercise of the power of appropriation shall also be the value at the date of the death.

22.3 Valuations made under this clause shall be binding upon all Persons interested under the Trust if the Trustees have ascertained those values in accordance with the duty of care set out in section 1(1) of the Trustee Act 2000.

23 Relationships Unknown to Trustees

23.1 The Trustees may distribute Trust Property or income in accordance with the Trust but without having ascertained that there is no Person who is or may be entitled to any interest therein by virtue of a relationship unknown to the Trustees. A Trustee shall not be liable to such a Person unless, at the time of the distribution, the Trustee has knowledge of circumstances which call for enquiry.

23.2 This clause does not prejudice any right of any Person to follow property or income into the hands of any Person, other than a purchaser, who may have received it.

GUIDE FOR PRACTITIONERS, TESTATORS AND SETTLORS

to the *STEP Standard Provisions* (2nd Edition)

(These guidance notes do not form part of the *STEP Standard Provisions*.)

The first edition of the *STEP Standard Provisions* was issued in 1992. It was one of the first projects of the (then) newly formed STEP. Professor John Adams described the Provisions as "quite the most exciting development for private client Drafters for several decades," and Ralph Ray called them "an enormous asset."

Since the publication of the first edition, Trusts law has been changed considerably, in particular by the Trusts of Land and Appointment of Trustees Act 1996 and the Trustee Act 2000.

After extensive consultation, STEP published the second edition of the *Standard Provisions* in October 2011. Will Writers and Drafters of Trust Deeds could continue to use the first edition, but it is expected that the second edition of the *STEP Standard Provisions* will be the usual practice.

These Provisions are subject to the Provisions in the Will or Settlement; however, the intention is that the Drafter should rely on the complete *STEP Standard Provisions* rather than a patchwork.

This guide does not attempt a full explanation of the Provisions. For that, readers are referred to *Drafting Trusts and Will Trusts* by James Kessler QC and Leon Sartin (Sweet & Maxwell). It is intended to assist the experienced Drafter who is broadly familiar with the first edition and focuses on what has changed.

A guide to the use of the Provisions intended for use by less experienced Will Writers is in the course of preparation (see the reference on page 12 to a "Will Writers' Toolkit").

The most important change, which will need your attention when drafting or reviewing a document, is that you now have a choice:

- to incorporate the only "core" Provisions of the second edition, or
- to incorporate the fuller form, which includes the "Special Provisions."

The Special Provisions are Provisions 14–23 and can be incorporated only by reference to them.

Clause 1 sets out forms of standard wording to incorporate the Provisions.

The second edition includes several additions to the first edition.

Clause 3(10) in the *STEP Standard Provisions* (first edition) has been deleted. This clause gave Trustees powers of insurance, which is now unnecessary as the general law has conferred an adequate statutory power of insurance.

These notes are intended to assist Practitioners, Settlors, and Testators in the use of the *STEP Standard Provisions*. They are not, and cannot be a substitute:

- as far as Practitioners are concerned, for careful consideration of the appropriateness, in the circumstances, of each Provision; and

EXECUTIVE SUMMARY

A Testator or Settlor should be aware of every term of his/her Will or Trust Deed, including those incorporated by reference through the *STEP Standard Provisions*, but some may feel that they lack the time or interest to consider every Provision and wish to leave it to their advisors.

The most important and possibly contentious elements of the *STEP Standard Provisions*, on which even the busiest Testator or Settlor should be informed, are as follows:

9 Conflicts of interest

10 Trustee remunerations

12 Liability of Trustees

Within the *STEP Special Provisions*, Testators and Settlors should pay particular attention to:

21 Powers relating to income and capital

Survivorship Clauses

The *STEP Standard Provisions* do not include a survivorship clause. There may be reasons, in particular affecting the transferable nil rate band, not to include such a clause, and if it is to be included, it must be expressed in the Will.

DETAILED GUIDANCE

STEP Standard Provisions (not Special Provisions): 1–13

1 Should you incorporate just the Standard Provisions or the Special Provisions as well?

This issue is fundamental to the approval of the second edition. See the comments above. The default choice is the Standard Provisions (excluding the Special Provisions), i.e., incorporating Provisions 1– 13 only.

2 Definitions

These set out terms that are used in the Provisions.

3 Protection for interest in Possession Trusts

This clause prevents accidental loss of IHT advantages, which is particularly important for "immediate post-death interests" under Wills.

4 Additional Powers

4.1 Investment

This clause confers a wide power of investment. In particular, Trustees may invest in land in any part of the world and in unsecured loans.

Provision 4.1 does not override the standard duties of investment in section 4 of the Trustee Act 2000, which provides:

(1) In exercising any power of investment, whether arising under this part or otherwise, a Trustee must have regard to the standard investment criteria.

(2) A Trustee must, from time to time, review the investments of the Trust and consider whether, having regard to the standard investment criteria, they should be varied.

(3) The standard investment criteria in relation to a Trust are:

(a) the suitability to the Trust of investments of the same kind as any particular investment proposed to be made or retained and of that particular investment as an investment of that kind, and

(b) the need for diversification of investments of the Trust, insofar as is appropriate to the circumstances of the Trust.

4.2 Management

Trustees have wide powers in the management of a property as if they owned it for themselves. This gives them the power to repair, maintain it, develop, or improve it.

4.3 Joint property

This clause confers a useful power to mix Trust Property with non- Trust Property, for example, to purchase a house for young Beneficiaries jointly with someone else, for example, their Guardian(s).

4.4 Income and capital

This provides that income may be set aside and invested to meet any liabilities that, in the opinion of the Trustees, ought to be borne out of income or to replace depreciation of the capital value of any Trust Property. In particular, income may be applied for a leasehold sinking-fund policy (a new power).

A Trustee must decide if and how much income to capitalise. Such consideration is not likely to cause controversy in relation to discretionary Trusts, where a Trustee normally has a discretion to distribute income and/or capital to the Beneficiaries or to accumulate. Trustees may experience more scrutiny in interest in Possession Trusts, where a life tenant may feel deprived of Trust income. A Trustee will have to consider the administrative burden of the additional work involved as well as the general duty to maintain the value of the Trust capital (holding a fair balance between life tenant and remainder man).

4.5 Accumulated income

The Provision speaks for itself. By virtue of the Perpetuities and Accumulations Act 2009, section 13, a power of accumulation may now exist for the entire perpetuity period of 125 years.

4.6 Use of Trust Property

Provision 4.6 gives the Trustees power to acquire any interest in property anywhere in the world for occupation or use by an Income Beneficiary on such terms as they see fit, without any of the restrictions on the rights of the Beneficiaries to occupy land under the Trust of Land and Appointment of Trustees Act 1996.

4.7 Application of Trust capital

Only the Trust instrument will determine exactly what powers the Trustees have, as this Provision is administrative, not dispositive: "how" the Trust Fund is used, rather than "who gets what." Thus Provision 4.7 will apply only if the Trustees have power to transfer capital to an Income Beneficiary. Assuming that the Trustees have the necessary power in the Trust document, they then have wide powers to deal with Trust capital, which includes advancing capital to an Income Beneficiary to augment their income.

4.8 Trade

This Provision is the same as in the first edition and gives Trustees the power to carry on trade in any part of the world, whether alone or in partnership.

4.9 Deposit of documents

Trustees continue to have the power to deposit documents relating to the Trust with any person.

4.10 Nominees

The power of Trustees to vest Trust Property in any Person as nominee has been extended to include sub-nominees.

4.11 Place of administration

4.12 Payment of tax

4.13 Indemnities

4.14 Security

These four provisions are self-explanatory and all appeared in the first edition.

4.15 Power of appropriation

The Trustees may appropriate Trust Property to any Person or class of Persons in or towards the satisfaction of their interest in the Trust Fund without the consent of the Beneficiary. This power is wider than the statutory power of appropriation in section 41 of the

Administration of Estates Act 1925, under which the consent of the Beneficiary is required.

This is the "basic" power of appropriation, available in all cases: a fuller power, set out in Special Provision 22, will be included if the Special Provisions apply.

4.16 Receipt by charities, etc.

This Provision has been extended to give the Trustees more protection than before, in that a Trustee is not to be liable for making a payment to any person who appears to be the treasurer or appropriate officer unless at the time of the distribution the Trustee has knowledge of circumstances which call for enquiry.

A new Provision provides that if any charity ceases to exist, changes its name, or enters into insolvent liquidation, before the time that the gift to the charity takes effect in possession (for example, between the signing of a Will and the death of the Testator), the gift shall instead be paid to such charity as the Trustees decide, having regard to the objects that were intended to benefit.

4. 17 Release of powers

This power may be used, for example, to remove a person from benefit under a discretionary Trust and so to exclude him.

4.18 Ancillary powers

This "catch-all" provision allows the Trustees to do what is necessary as part of their duties even where the power is not specifically set out.

5 Powers of Maintenance and Advancement

Provision 5 modifies sections 31 and 32 of the Trustee Act 1925. The proviso in section 31(1) of the Trustee Act 1925 requires Trustees, in exercising their discretion in favour of any minor Beneficiary, to have regard to any other income available for the minor's maintenance and use a proportionate part of each fund. As this may not be convenient, the proviso has been deleted.

Section 32(2) of the Trustee Act 1925, in its unlamented form, confers the power of Trustees to advance capital up to one-half of the presumptive or vested share or interest of a Beneficiary. This restriction is removed by Provision 5.2, so it allows a Trustee to advance the whole, rather than one half. This is in line with general practice.

6 Minors and Beneficiaries Without Capacity: Powers Over Income

This Provision provides that income for the benefit of a minor may be paid either to the minor's parent or Guardian on behalf of the minor until the minor has reached the age of 16or to the minor after attaining that age. The Trustees are under no duty to enquire into the use of the income unless they have knowledge of circumstances which call for enquiry. There is a similar power over capital but, being more important and perhaps not always wanted, this appears as Special Provision 18 below.

The power may also be exercised in a way that may limit dissipation of money by, in effect, "earmarking" funds, holding them as bare Trustee for the young Beneficiary pending coming of age. That may secure the tax advantages of receipt by the young person of income against which the personal allowance may be set while avoiding youthful excess, with funds actually being released at age 18.

Provision 6.3 further provides that, in the absence of a Lasting Power of Attorney, Trustees may apply any income for the benefit of a Beneficiary who lacks mental capacity at their discretion, subject to the direction of the court or directions of a deputy appointed under the Mental Capacity Act 2005.

Any such payments of capital or income can be made to the Person having or appearing to the Trustees to have the care and financial responsibility of such Person. There is no duty on the Trustees to enquire into the use of the income or capital unless they have knowledge of circumstances which call forenquiry.

7 Disclaimer

This Provision speaks for itself: the ability to disclaim only part of a gift adds flexibility.

8 Apportionment

No apportionment is required of income or expenditure. This saves costs without creating significant unfairness. This removes the need for detailed, expensive calculations where the administrative cost may exceed the sums in issue. This will facilitate the administration of an estate.

9 Conflicts of Interest

Under this Provision, an Independent Trustee is needed in situations where there is a conflict of interest between the Fiduciary duties of anyone who owes a duty to the Trust and their personal interest or other duties. In relation to administrative matters, and once the conflict has been disclosed to the Trustees, an Independent Trustee is required to consider whether the matter conflicts with the interests of the Trust.

An Independent Trustee is also required if the powers are used to benefit a Trustee – unless the Trustees are still the Trustees as originally appointed. (The exception is new.)

Provision 9.1.2 excludes certain people from qualifying as Independent Trustees.

10 Trustee Remunerations

This Provision has been cut down in the second edition to entitle only Trustees acting in their professional capacity to be remunerated for their services. There must now be a link between the skill set of the Trustee and the work actually done.

Provision 10 no longer specifically provides that Trustees can charge for work that does not require professional assistance, as this is now covered by section 28 of the Trustee Act 2000 and is therefore superfluous.

The current drafting is based on the statutory Provisions in section 29 of the Trustee Act 2000 and is sufficient to entitle a Trustee to recover reasonable remuneration for services provided in a professional capacity or any partnership or LLP of which the Trustee is a member. It is considered that section 29 of the Trustee Act 2000 is wide enough to allow a partnership or LLP to charge.

11 Trust Corporations

Where a Trust Corporation is appointed as Trustee, the Trust Corporation may act on the standard terms of engagement of the Trust Corporation as published at the date of the execution of the Will or Settlement.

Provision 11.2 is new and may help where a Trust Corporation is appointed Trustee many years after the Deed was executed that incorporated these Provisions. On the appointment of a Trust Corporation, the Trust Corporation may rely on the standard terms of engagement published on the date of the appointment. The Person making the appointment has the opportunity to review those terms and, if not satisfied, need not make the appointment.

If there is a conflict between the terms of engagement of the Trust Corporation and the Standard Provisions, the terms of engagement shall prevail.

12 Liability of Trustees

Trustees are not liable for breach of Trust when they have acted honestly and with reasonable care. This clause also relieves a lay Trustee, even if negligent, unless guilty of fraud and as long as there is a professional Trustee. This is consistent with STEP and Law Commission guidance. Thus, a lay Trustee may, if they choose, broadly leave the Trust administration to a professional co-Trustee.

It also provides that a Trustee shall not be liable for breach of Trust when acting upon advice from counsel of at least five years standing, unless:

- the Trustee knows or suspects that counsel's instructions were incomplete
- court proceedings are pending on the matter
- the Trustee has a personal interest in the matter, or
- the Trustee committed a breach of Trust in the subject matter of the advice
- a Trustee may distribute Trust Property to a Beneficiary for as long as they have no knowledge of another Person's prior or concurrent interest.

13 Subsequent Editions of STEP Standard Provisions

It is not proposed to bring out new editions of the *STEP Standard Provisions* often, but at some time, a third edition may be needed. The Trustees may by Deed incorporate that or any subsequent edition of the *STEP Standard Provisions*. Any such incorporation will, however, be subject to the provisions in the Principal Document. It is considered, in the light of Re Beatty [1990] 1 WLR 1503, that later editions may be incorporated in this way.

Most importantly, if the Special Provisions 14–23 (see below) have not been incorporated in the Principal Document, the Trustees cannot incorporate them at a later stage.

STEP Special Provisions: 14-23

14 Borrowing

This clause has been taken from the first edition without amendment but was felt to be far-reaching and is therefore included in the Special Provisions. Trustees may borrow money for investment or any other purpose.

15 Delegation

Provision 15, which provides that a Trustee may delegate in writing any of their functions to any Person, includes a Provision that none of the restrictions in sections 12–15 of the Trustee Act 2000 shall apply.

Under the *STEP Standard Provisions*, there is no obligation to consult with Beneficiaries when deciding to delegate any of their functions. Therefore, a delegate can make decisions without consulting either the delegating Trustee or the Beneficiaries. Normally a Beneficiary should be consulted.

16 Supervision of Company

This Provision is deemed "special" because it absolves Trustees from an important duty they would otherwise have, particularly in relation to unquoted family companies.

A Trustee may distribute Trust Property to a Beneficiary for as long as they have no knowledge of another Person's prior or concurrent interest.

17 Powers of Maintenance: Deferring Income Entitlement to 21

If section 31 of the Trustee Act 1925 applies, a Beneficiary becomes entitled to Trust income at the age of 18. This has been modified: A Beneficiary becomes entitled to Trust income at the Specified Age, which is the age of 21 years or such earlier years as the Trustees by Deed specify, for as long as the Specified Age is not less than 18 years. This would allow Trustees to defer entitlement to income to the age of 21.

18 Minors and Beneficiaries Without Capacity: Powers Over Trust Capital

This Provision mirrors Standard Provision 6 relating to income. It provides that capital held for the benefit of a minor may be paid to the minor's parent or Guardian on behalf of the minor until the minor has reached the age of 16. The Trustees are under no duty to enquire into the use of the income or capital unless they have knowledge of circumstances that call for an enquiry.

This extends the powers in the first edition in that capital can be paid for the benefit of the minor rather than income only.

Provision 18.2 further provides that, in the absence of a Lasting Power of Attorney, Trustees may apply any capital for the benefit of a Beneficiary who lacks mental capacity at their discretion, subject to the direction of the court's or directions of a deputy appointed under the Mental Capacity Act 2005.

Any such payments of capital can be made to the Person having or appearing to the Trustees to have the care and financial responsibility of such Person. Again, there is no duty on the Trustees to enquire into the use of the income or capital unless they have knowledge of circumstances which call for enquiry.

19 Absolute Discretion Clause

For the avoidance of doubt and to disapply the Trust of Land and Appointment of Trustees Act 1996, section 11, this Provision allows Trustees to exercise their discretion freely and without supervision by the Beneficiaries.

20 Appointment and Retirement of Trustees

This Provision allows the appointment of offshore Trustees.

The first edition referred to a retirement age of 65, but to reflect current thinking, this has been removed in the second edition to allow Trustees to act beyond the age of 65.

Provision 20.2 addresses the situation where a Trustee wishes to retire even though that will leave only one Person left to act. It allows a Trustee to retire in these circumstances, leaving a sole Trustee, not necessarily a Trust Corporation, to continue administering the Trust. It will be for the continuing Trustee to weigh the arguments for and against allowing a retirement in these circumstances, which for a small Trust could save expense.

21 Powers Relating to Income and Capital

This expressly overrides the Trustees' duty to balance the interests of the Beneficiaries. This power, for example, can be used to reduce the income of a life tenant in favour of the remainder man. It also gives the Trustees wider powers of investment in that they can acquire and retain wasting assets and assets which yield little income. They may also acquiesce in management for example of to a private company, even though their shareholding may produce no income. Trustees should bear in mind that favouring income interests over capital may, in the long run, disadvantage both.

22 Power to Appropriate at Value at Time of Death

This enables the Trustees to appropriate assets at value at time of death rather than at the time of the appropriation. This is considered to be an administrative power. It may sometimes have tax advantages.

This provision gives Trustees discretion that should be explained to the client when deciding whether to include this particular Special Provision. There is protection for Beneficiaries in that the Trustees must take reasonable care when ascertaining values for appropriation.

23 Relationships Unknown to Trustees

While Trustees must take care, they may distribute Trust Property on the basis of what they actually know, even though other Beneficiaries may exist by virtue of family connections hidden from, or not disclosed to, the Trustees.

STEP Will writers' Toolkit

STEP is keen to promote the use of the STEP Standard Provisions where they suit the circumstances of the client and provided that the drafter has full knowledge of them and of how to use them. With that in mind, STEP intends to produce a further guide to their use, including a form of letter suitable to send to clients highlighting the most important provisions and setting them out in full. The further guide will comment on certain parts of the Provisions that caused the greatest deliberation in arriving at the agreed form of the second edition.

APPENDIX VII

LASTING POWER OF ATTORNEY
(FINANCIAL DECISIONS)

Office of the
Public Guardian

Lasting power
of attorney

Financial decisions

Registering
an LPA costs

£82

This fee is means-tested:
see the application
Guide part B

Use this for:

- running your bank and savings accounts
- making or selling investments
- paying your bills
- buying or selling your house

How to complete this form

PLEASE WRITE IN CAPITAL LETTERS USING A BLACK PEN

☒ Mark your choice with an X

■ If you make a mistake, fill in the box and then mark the correct
choice with an X

Don't use correction fluid. Cross out mistakes and rewrite nearby.
Everyone involved in each section must initial each change.

Making an LPA online is simpler, clearer and faster

Our smart online form gives you just the right amount of help
exactly when you need it: **www.gov.uk/power-of-attorney**

Before
you start...

This form is also available in Welsh. Call the helpline on 0300 456 0300.

The people involved in your LPA

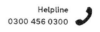

You'll find it easier to make an LPA if you first choose the people you want to help you. **Note their names here now** so you can refer back later.

People you must have to make an LPA

Donor

If you are filling this form in for yourself, you are the donor. If you are filling this in for a friend or relative, they are the donor.

Attorneys

Attorneys are the people you pick to make decisions for you. They don't need legal training.

They should be people you trust and know well; for example, your husband, wife, partner, adult children or good friends.

Choose one attorney or more. If you have a lot, they might find it hard to make decisions together.

Certificate provider

You need someone to confirm that no one is forcing you to make an LPA and you understand what you are doing. This is your 'certificate provider'. They must either:

- have relevant professional skills, such as a doctor or lawyer
- have known you well for at least two years, such as a friend or colleague

Some people can't be a certificate provider. See the list in the Guide, part A10.

Witnesses

You can't witness your attorneys' signatures and they can't witness yours. Anyone else over 18 years old can be a witness.

People you might want to include in your LPA

Replacement attorneys

You don't have to appoint replacement attorneys but they help protect your LPA. Without them, your LPA might not work if one of your original attorneys stops acting for you.

People to notify

'People to notify' add security. They can raise concerns about your LPA before it's registered – for example, if they think you are under pressure to make the LPA.

This page is not part of the form

LP1F Property and
financial affairs (03.17)

203

Office of the
Public Guardian

Lasting power of attorney for property and financial affairs

Section 1
The donor

You are appointing other people to make decisions on your behalf.
You are 'the donor'.

Restrictions – you must be at least 18 years old and be able to understand and make decisions for yourself (called 'mental capacity').

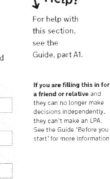

Help?

For help with
this section,
see the
Guide, part A1.

If you are filling this in for a friend or relative and they can no longer make decisions independently, they can't make an LPA. See the Guide 'Before you start' for more information.

Title   First names

Last name

Any other names you're known by (optional – eg your married name)

Date of birth

Day   Month   Year

Address

Postcode

Email address (optional)

For OPG office use only

LPA registration date   OPG reference number

Day   Month   Year

Only valid with the official stamp here.

LP1F Property and financial
affairs (07.15)

1

204

Section 2
The attorneys

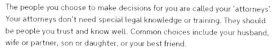

The people you choose to make decisions for you are called your 'attorneys'. Your attorneys don't need special legal knowledge or training. They should be people you trust and know well. Common choices include your husband, wife or partner, son or daughter, or your best friend.

You need at least one attorney, but you can have more.

You'll also be able to choose 'replacement attorneys' in section 4. They can step in if one of the attorneys you appoint here can no longer act for you.

To appoint a trust corporation, fill in the first attorney space and tick the box in that section. They must sign Continuation sheet 4. For more about trust corporations, see the Guide, part A2.

 Help?

Restrictions – Attorneys must be at least 18 years old and must have mental capacity to make decisions. They must not be bankrupt or subject to a debt relief order.

For help with this section, see the Guide, part A2.

Title	First names		Title	First names

Last name (or trust corporation name)

Last name

Date of birth

Day   Month   Year

Date of birth

Day   Month   Year

Address

Address

Postcode

Postcode

Email address (optional)

Email address (optional)

☐ This attorney is a trust corporation.

205

Title   First names

Last name

Date of birth

Day   Month   Year

Address

Postcode

Email address (optional)

Title   First names

Last name

Date of birth

Day   Month   Year

Address

Postcode

Email address (optional)

More attorneys – I want to appoint more than 4 attorneys. Use Continuation sheet 1.

206

Section 3

How should your attorneys make decisions?

You need to choose whether your attorneys can make decisions on their own or must agree some or all decisions unanimously.

Whatever you choose, they must always act in your best interests.

☐ **I only appointed one attorney** (turn to section 4)

How do you want your attorneys to work together? (tick one only)

☐ **Jointly and severally**

Attorneys can make decisions on their own or together. Most people choose this option because it's the most practical. Attorneys can get together to make important decisions if they wish, but can make simple or urgent decisions on their own. It's up to the attorneys to choose when they act together or alone. It also means that if one of the attorneys dies or can no longer act, your LPA will still work.

If one attorney makes a decision, it has the same effect as if all the attorneys made that decision.

☐ **Jointly**

Attorneys must agree unanimously on every decision, however big or small. Remember, some simple decisions could be delayed because it takes time to get the attorneys together. If your attorneys can't agree a decision, then they can only make that decision by going to court.

Be careful – if one attorney dies or can no longer act, all your attorneys become unable to act. This is because the law says a group appointed 'jointly' is a single unit. Your LPA will stop working unless you appoint at least one replacement attorney (in section 4).

☐ **Jointly for some decisions, jointly and severally for other decisions**

Attorneys must agree unanimously on some decisions, but can make others on their own. If you choose this option, you must list the decisions your attorneys should make jointly and agree unanimously on Continuation sheet 2. The wording you use is important. There are examples in the Guide, part A3.

Be careful – if one attorney dies or can no longer act, none of your attorneys will be able to make any of the decisions you've said should be made jointly. Your LPA will stop working for those decisions unless you appoint at least one replacement attorney (in section 4). Your original attorneys will still be able to make any of the other decisions alongside your replacement attorneys.

Help?

For help with this section, see the Guide, part A3.

If you choose 'jointly for some decisions...', you may want to take legal advice, particularly if the examples in part A3 of the the Guide, don't match your needs.

207

Section 4
Replacement attorneys

This section is optional, but we recommend you consider it

Replacement attorneys are a backup in case one of your original attorneys can't make decisions for you any more.

To appoint a trust corporation, fill in the first attorney space below and tick the box in that section. They must sign Continuation sheet 4.

Reasons replacement attorneys step in – if one of your original attorneys dies, loses capacity, no longer wants to be your attorney, becomes bankrupt or subject to a debt relief order or is no longer legally your husband, wife or civil partner.

Restrictions – replacement attorneys must be at least 18 years old and have mental capacity to make decisions. They must not be bankrupt or subject to a debt relief order.

Help?

For help with this section, see the Guide, part A4.

Title	First names		Title	First names

Last name (or trust corporation name)

Last name

Date of birth

Day   Month   Year

Date of birth

Day   Month   Year

Address

Address

Postcode

Postcode

☐ This attorney is a trust corporation.

☐ **More replacements** – I want to appoint more than two replacements. Use Continuation sheet 1.

When and how your replacement attorneys can act

Replacement attorneys usually step in when one of your **original** attorneys stops acting for you. If there's more than one **replacement** attorney, they will all step in at once. If they **fully** replace your original attorney(s) at once, they will usually act jointly. You can change some aspects of this, but most people don't. See the Guide, part A4.

You should consider taking legal advice if you want to change when or how your replacement attorneys act.

☐ I want to change when or how my attorneys can act (optional). Use Continuation sheet 2.

208

Section 5
When can your attorneys make decisions?

You can allow your attorneys to make decisions:
• as soon as the LPA has been registered by the Office of the Public Guardian
• only when you don't have mental capacity

While you have mental capacity you will be in control of all decisions affecting you. If you choose the first option, your attorneys can only make decisions on your behalf if you allow them to. They are responsible to you for any decisions you let them make.

Your attorneys must always act in your best interests.

When do you want your attorneys to be able to make decisions?
(mark one only)

Help?

For help with this section, see the Guide, part A5.

☐ **As soon as my LPA has been registered**
(and also when I don't have mental capacity)

Most people choose this option because it is the most practical.

While you still have mental capacity, your attorneys can only act **with your consent**. If you later lose capacity, they can continue to act on your behalf for all decisions covered by this LPA.

This option is useful if you are able to make your own decisions but there's another reason you want your attorneys to help you – for example, if you're away on holiday, or if you have a physical condition that makes it difficult to visit the bank, talk on the phone or sign documents.

☐ **Only when I don't have mental capacity**

Be careful – this can make your LPA a lot less useful. Your attorneys might be asked to prove you do not have mental capacity each time they try to use this LPA.

209

Section 6
People to notify when the LPA is registered

This section is optional

You can let people know that you're going to register your LPA. They can raise any concerns they have about the LPA – for example, if there was any pressure or fraud in making it.

When the LPA is registered, the person applying to register (you or one of your attorneys) must send a notice to each 'person to notify'.

You can't put your attorneys or replacement attorneys here.

People to notify can object to the LPA, but only for certain reasons (listed in the notification form LP3). After that, they are no longer involved in the LPA. Choose people who care about your best interests and who would be willing to speak up if they were concerned.

Help?

For help with this section, see the Guide, part A6.

Title	First names		Title	First names

Last name

Last name

Address

Address

Postcode

Postcode

Title	First names		Title	First names

Last name

Last name

Address

Address

Postcode

Postcode

☐ I want to appoint another person to notify (maximum is 5) – use Continuation sheet 1.

Only valid with the official stamp here.

LP1F Property and financial affairs (07.15)

7

210

Section 7
Preferences and instructions

This section is optional

You can tell your attorneys how you'd **prefer** them to make decisions, or give them specific **instructions** which they must follow when making decisions.

Most people leave this page blank – you can just talk to your attorneys so they understand how you want them to make decisions for you.

Help?

For help with this section, see the Guide, part A7.

Preferences

Your attorneys don't have to follow your preferences but they should keep them in mind. For examples of preferences, see the Guide, part A7.

Preferences – use words like 'prefer' and 'would like'

☐ I need more space – use Continuation sheet 2.

Instructions

Your attorneys will have to follow your instructions exactly. For examples of instructions, see the Guide, part A7.

Be careful – if you give instructions that are not legally correct they would have to be removed before your LPA could be registered.

If you want to give instructions, you may want to take legal advice.

Instructions – use words like 'must' and 'have to'

☐ I need more space – use Continuation sheet 2.

Only valid with the official stamp here.

211

Section 8
Your legal rights and responsibilities

 Everyone signing the LPA must read this information

In sections 9 to 11, you, the certificate provider, all your attorneys and your replacement attorneys must sign this lasting power of attorney to form a legal agreement between you (a deed).

By signing this lasting power of attorney, you (the donor) are appointing people (attorneys) to make decisions for you.

LPAs are governed by the Mental Capacity Act 2005 (MCA), regulations made under it and the MCA Code of Practice. Attorneys must have regard to these documents. The Code of Practice is available from www.gov.uk/opg/mca-code or from The Stationery Office.

Your attorneys must follow the principles of the Mental Capacity Act:

1. Your attorneys must assume that you can make your own decisions unless it is established that you cannot do so.
2. Your attorneys must help you to make as many of your own decisions as you can. They must take all practical steps to help you to make a decision. They can only treat you as unable to make a decision if they have not succeeded in helping you make a decision through those steps.
3. Your attorneys must not treat you as unable to make a decision simply because you make an unwise decision.
4. Your attorneys must act and make decisions in your best interests when you are unable to make a decision.
5. Before your attorneys make a decision or act for you, they must consider whether they can make the decision or act in a way that is less restrictive of your rights and freedom but still achieves the purpose.

Your attorneys must always act in your best interests. This is explained in the Application guide, part A8, and defined in the MCA Code of Practice.

Before this LPA can be used:
• it must be registered by the Office of the Public Guardian (OPG)
• it may be limited to when you don't have mental capacity, according to your choice in section 5

Cancelling your LPA: You can cancel this LPA at any time, as long as you have mental capacity to do so. It doesn't matter if the LPA has been registered or not. For more information, see the Guide, part D.

Your will and your LPA: Your attorneys cannot use this LPA to change your will. This LPA will expire when you die. Your attorneys must then send the registered LPA, any certified copies and a copy of your death certificate to the Office of the Public Guardian.

Data protection: For information about how OPG uses your personal data, see the Guide, part D.

Help?

For help with this section, see the Guide, part A8.

Only valid with the official stamp here.

LP1F Property and financial affairs (07.15)

9

Section 9
Signature: donor

By signing on this page I confirm all of the following:

- I have read this lasting power of attorney (LPA) including section 8 'Your legal rights and responsibilities', or I have had it read to me

- I appoint and give my attorneys authority to make decisions about my property and financial affairs, including when I cannot act for myself because I lack mental capacity, subject to the terms of this LPA and to the provisions of the Mental Capacity Act 2005

- I have either appointed people to notify (in section 6) or I have chosen not to notify anyone when the LPA is registered

- I agree to the information I've provided being used by the Office of the Public Guardian in carrying out its duties

Be careful

Sign this page (and any continuation sheets) before anyone signs sections 10 and 11.

Donor

Signed (or marked) by the person giving this lasting power of attorney and delivered as a deed.

Signature or mark

Date signed or marked

Day   Month   Year

If you have used Continuation sheets 1 or 2 you must sign and date each continuation sheet at the same time as you sign this page.

If you can't sign this LPA you can make a mark instead. If you can't sign or make a mark you can instruct someone else to sign for you, using Continuation sheet 3.

Witness

The witness must not be an attorney or replacement attorney appointed under this LPA, and must be aged 18 or over.

Signature or mark

Full name of witness

Address

Postcode

Help? For help with this section, see the Guide, part A9.

213

Section 10
Signature: certificate provider

 Only sign this section after the donor has signed section 9

The 'certificate provider' signs to confirm they've discussed the lasting power of attorney (LPA) with the donor, that the donor understands what they're doing and that nobody is forcing them to do it. The 'certificate provider' should be either:

Help?

For help with this section, see the Guide, part A10.

- someone who has known the donor personally for at least 2 years, such as a friend, neighbour, colleague or former colleague
- someone with relevant professional skills, such as the donor's GP, a healthcare professional or a solicitor

A certificate provider **can't** be one of the attorneys.

Certificate provider's statement

I certify that, as far as I'm aware, at the time of signing section 9:

- the donor understood the purpose of this LPA and the scope of the authority conferred under it
- no fraud or undue pressure is being used to induce the donor to create this LPA
- there is nothing else which would prevent this LPA from being created by the completion of this instrument

By signing this section I confirm that:

- I am aged 18 or over
- I have read this LPA, including section 8 'Your legal rights and responsibilities'
- there is no restriction on my acting as a certificate provider
- the donor has chosen me as someone who has known them personally for at least 2 years **OR**
- the donor has chosen me as a person with relevant professional skills and expertise

Restrictions – the certificate provider must not be:

- an attorney or replacement attorney named in this LPA or any other LPA or enduring power of attorney for the donor
- a member of the donor's family or of one of the attorneys' families, including husbands, wives, civil partners, in-laws and step-relatives
- an unmarried partner, boyfriend or girlfriend of either the donor or one of the attorneys (whether or not they live at the same address)
- the donor's or an attorney's business partner
- the donor's or an attorney's employee
- an owner, manager, director or employee of a care home where the donor lives

Certificate provider

Title   First names

Last name

Address

Postcode

Signature or mark

Date signed or marked

Day   Month   Year

Only valid with the official stamp here.

LP1F Property and financial affairs (07.15)

11

Section 11

Signature: attorney or replacement

 Only sign this section after the certificate provider has signed section 10

All the attorneys and replacement attorneys need to sign.
There are 4 copies of this page – make more copies if you need to.

Help?

For help with this section, see the Guide, part A11.

By signing this section I understand and confirm all of the following:

- I am aged 18 or over

- I have read this lasting power of attorney (LPA) including section 8 'Your legal rights and responsibilities', or I have had it read to me

- I have a duty to act based on the principles of the Mental Capacity Act 2005 and to have regard to the Mental Capacity Act Code of Practice

- I must make decisions and act in the best interests of the donor

- I must take into account any instructions or preferences set out in this LPA

- I can make decisions and act only when this LPA has been registered and at the time indicated in section 5 of this LPA

Further statement by a replacement attorney: I understand that I have the authority to act under this LPA only after an original attorney's appointment is terminated. I must notify the Public Guardian if this happens.

Attorney or replacement attorney	**Witness**
Signed (or marked) by the attorney or replacement attorney and delivered as a deed.	The witness must not be the donor of this LPA, and must be aged 18 or over.

Signature or mark	Signature or mark

Date signed or marked

Day   Month   Year

Title   First names

Full names of witness

Address

Last name

Postcode

215

Section 11
Signature: attorney or replacement

 Only sign this section after the certificate provider has signed section 10

All the attorneys and replacement attorneys need to sign.
There are 4 copies of this page – make more copies if you need to.

Help?

For help with this section, see the Guide, part A11.

By signing this section I understand and confirm all of the following:

• I am aged 18 or over

• I have read this lasting power of attorney (LPA) including section 8 'Your legal rights and responsibilities', or I have had it read to me

• I have a duty to act based on the principles of the Mental Capacity Act 2005 and to have regard to the Mental Capacity Act Code of Practice

• I must make decisions and act in the best interests of the donor

• I must take into account any instructions or preferences set out in this LPA

• I can make decisions and act only when this LPA has been registered and at the time indicated in section 5 of this LPA

Further statement by a replacement attorney: I understand that I have the authority to act under this LPA only after an original attorney's appointment is terminated. I must notify the Public Guardian if this happens.

Attorney or replacement attorney	Witness
Signed (or marked) by the attorney or replacement attorney and delivered as a deed.	The witness must not be the donor of this LPA, and must be aged 18 or over.
Signature or mark	Signature or mark
Date signed or marked	Full names of witness
Day Month Year	Address
Title First names	
Last name	Postcode

Only valid with the official stamp here.

LP1F Property and financial affairs (07.15)

13

Section 11

Signature: attorney or replacement

 Only sign this section after the certificate provider has signed section 10

All the attorneys and replacement attorneys need to sign.
There are 4 copies of this page – make more copies if you need to.

By signing this section I understand and confirm all of the following:

- I am aged 18 or over
- I have read this lasting power of attorney (LPA) including section 8 'Your legal rights and responsibilities', or I have had it read to me
- I have a duty to act based on the principles of the Mental Capacity Act 2005 and to have regard to the Mental Capacity Act Code of Practice
- I must make decisions and act in the best interests of the donor
- I must take into account any instructions or preferences set out in this LPA
- I can make decisions and act only when this LPA has been registered and at the time indicated in section 5 of this LPA

Further statement by a replacement attorney: I understand that I have the authority to act under this LPA only after an original attorney's appointment is terminated. I must notify the Public Guardian if this happens.

Help?

For help with this section, see the Guide, part A11.

Attorney or replacement attorney	Witness
Signed (or marked) by the attorney or replacement attorney and delivered as a deed.	The witness must not be the donor of this LPA, and must be aged 18 or over.

Attorney or replacement attorney

Signed (or marked) by the attorney or replacement attorney and delivered as a deed.

Signature or mark

Date signed or marked

Day   Month   Year

Title   First names

Last name

Witness

The witness must not be the donor of this LPA, and must be aged 18 or over.

Signature or mark

Full names of witness

Address

Postcode

Only valid with the official stamp here.

LP1F Property and financial affairs (07.15)

14

Section 11
Signature: attorney or replacement

 Only sign this section after the certificate provider has signed section 10

All the attorneys and replacement attorneys need to sign.
There are 4 copies of this page – make more copies if you need to.

By signing this section I understand and confirm all of the following:

• I am aged 18 or over

• I have read this lasting power of attorney (LPA) including section 8 'Your legal rights and responsibilities', or I have had it read to me

• I have a duty to act based on the principles of the Mental Capacity Act 2005 and to have regard to the Mental Capacity Act Code of Practice

• I must make decisions and act in the best interests of the donor

• I must take into account any instructions or preferences set out in this LPA

• I can make decisions and act only when this LPA has been registered and at the time indicated in section 5 of this LPA

Further statement by a replacement attorney: I understand that I have the authority to act under this LPA only after an original attorney's appointment is terminated. I must notify the Public Guardian if this happens.

Help?

For help with this section, see the Guide, part A11.

Attorney or replacement attorney

Signed (or marked) by the attorney or replacement attorney and delivered as a deed.

Signature or mark

Date signed or marked

Day   Month   Year

Title   First names

Last name

Witness

The witness must not be the donor of this LPA, and must be aged 18 or over.

Signature or mark

Full names of witness

Address

Postcode

218

Now register your LPA

Before the LPA can be used, it **must** be registered by the Office of the Public Guardian (OPG). Continue filling in this form to register the LPA. See part B of the Guide.

People to notify

If there are any 'people to notify' listed in section 6, you must notify them that you are registering the LPA now. See part C of the Guide.

Fill in and send each of them a copy of the form to notify people – LP3.

When you sign section 15 of this form, you are confirming that you've sent forms to the 'people to notify'.

Register now

You do not have to register immediately, but it's a good idea in case you've made any mistakes. If you delay until after the donor loses mental capacity, it will be impossible to fix any errors. This could make the whole LPA invalid and it will not be possible to register or use it.

219

Register your lasting power of attorney

Section 12
The applicant

You can only apply to register if you are either the donor or attorney(s) for this LPA. The donor and attorney(s) should not apply together.

Who is applying to register the LPA? (tick one only)

☐ **Donor** – the donor needs to sign section 15

☐ **Attorney(s)** – If the attorneys were appointed jointly (in section 3) then they **all** need to sign section 15. Otherwise, only one of the attorneys needs to sign

Help?

For help with this section, see the Guide, part B2.

Write the name and date of birth for each attorney that is applying to register the LPA. Don't include any attorneys who are not applying.

Title   First names

Last name

Date of birth

Day   Month   Year

Title   First names

Last name

Date of birth

Day   Month   Year

Title   First names

Last name

Date of birth

Day   Month   Year

Title   First names

Last name

Date of birth

Day   Month   Year

220

Section 13

Who do you want to receive the LPA?

We need to know who to send the LPA to once it is registered. We might also need to contact someone with questions about the application.

We already have the addresses of the donor and attorneys, so you don't have to repeat any of those here, unless they have changed.

Who would you like to receive the LPA and any correspondence?

☐ **The donor**

☐ **An attorney** (write name below)

☐ **Other** (write name and address below)

Title   First names

Last name

Company (optional)

Address

Postcode

How would the person above prefer to be contacted?

You can choose more than one.

☐ **Post**

☐ **Phone**

☐ **Email**

☐ **Welsh** (we will write to the person in Welsh)

Help?

For help with this section, see the Guide, part B3.

Section 14
Application fee

There's a fee for registering a lasting power of attorney – the amount is shown on the cover sheet of this form or on form LPA120.

The fee changes from time to time. You can check you are paying the correct amount at www.gov.uk/power-of-attorney/how-much-it-costs or call 0300 456 0300. The Office of the Public Guardian can't register your LPA until you have paid the fee.

How would you like to pay?

☐ **Card** For security, **don't** write your credit or debit card details here. We'll contact you to process the payment.

Your phone number

☐ **Cheque** Enclose a cheque with your application.

Help?

For help with this section, see the Guide, part B4.

Reduced application fee

If the donor has a low income, you may not have to pay the full amount. See the Guide, part B4 for details.

☐ **I want to apply to pay a reduced fee**

You'll need to fill in form LPA120 and include it with your application. You'll also **need to send proof** that the donor is eligible to pay a reduced fee.

Are you making a repeat application?

If you've already applied to register an LPA and the Office of the Public Guardian said that it was not possible to register it, you can apply again within 3 months and pay a reduced fee.

☐ **I'm making a repeat application**

Case number

For OPG office use only

Payment reference

Payment date   Amount

Day   Month   Year

Section 15
Signature

 Do not sign this section until after sections 9, 10 and 11 have been signed.

The person applying to register the LPA (see section 12) must sign and date this section. This is either the donor or attorney(s) but not both together.

If the **attorneys** are applying to register the LPA and they were appointed to act **jointly** (in section 3), they must all sign.

By signing this section I confirm the following:

- I apply to register the LPA that accompanies this application
- I have informed 'people to notify' named in section 6 of the LPA (if any) of my intention to register the LPA
- I certify that the information in this form is correct to the best of my knowledge and belief

Help?

For help with this section, see the Guide, part B5.

Signature or mark	Signature or mark

Date signed	Date signed
Day Month Year	Day Month Year

Signature or mark	Signature or mark

Date signed	Date signed
Day Month Year	Day Month Year

If more than 4 attorneys need to sign, make copies of this page.

223

Check your lasting power of attorney

You don't have to use this checklist, but it'll help you make sure you've completed your LPA correctly.

☐ The donor filled in sections 1 to 7.

☐ The donor signed section 9 in the presence of a witness. The donor also signed any copies of continuation sheets 1 and 2 that were used, on the same date as signing section 9.

☐ The certificate provider signed section 10.

☐ All the attorneys and replacement attorneys signed section 11, in the presence of witness(es).

☐ Sections 9, 10 and 11 were signed in order. Section 9 must have been signed first, then section 10, then section 11. They can be dated the same day or different days.

☐ The donor or an attorney completed sections 12 to 15. If the attorneys are applying and were appointed 'jointly' (section 3), they have all signed section 15 of this form.

☐ I've paid the application fee or applied for a reduced fee. If I've applied for a reduced fee, I've included the required evidence and completed form LPA120A.

☐ If there were any people to notify in section 6, I've notified them using form LP3.

☐ I've not left out any of the pages of the LPA, even the ones where I didn't write anything or there were no boxes to fill in.

Helpline
0300 456 0300

Send to:

Office of the Public Guardian
PO Box 16185
Birmingham B2 2WH

This page is not part of the form

LP1F Property and
financial affairs (03.17)

APPENDIX VIII

LASTING POWER OF ATTORNEY
(HEALTH AND CARE DECISIONS)

Office of the
Public Guardian

Lasting power
of attorney

Health and care
decisions

**Registering
an LPA costs**

£82
This fee is means-tested:
see the application
Guide part B

Use this for:

- the type of health care and medical treatment you
  receive, including life-sustaining treatment
- where you live
- day-to-day matters such as your diet and daily routine

How to complete this form

PLEASE WRITE IN CAPITAL LETTERS USING A BLACK PEN

☒ Mark your choice with an X

■ If you make a mistake, fill in the box and then mark the correct
choice with an X

Don't use correction fluid. Cross out mistakes and rewrite nearby.
Everyone involved in each section must initial each change.

Making an LPA online is simpler, clearer and faster

Our smart online form gives you just the right amount of help
exactly when you need it: **www.gov.uk/power-of-attorney**

Before
you start...

This form is also available in Welsh. Call the helpline on 0300 456 0300.

The people involved in your LPA

You'll find it easier to make an LPA if you first choose the people you want to help you. **Note their names here now** so you can refer back later.

People you must have to make an LPA

Donor

If you are filling this form in for yourself, you are the donor. If you are filling this in for a friend or relative, they are the donor.

Attorneys

Attorneys are the people you pick to make decisions for you. They don't need legal training.

They should be people you trust and know well; for example, your husband, wife, partner, adult children or good friends.

Choose one attorney or more. If you have a lot, they might find it hard to make decisions together.

Certificate provider

You need someone to confirm that no one is forcing you to make an LPA and you understand what you are doing. This is your 'certificate provider'. They must either:

- have relevant professional skills, such as a doctor or lawyer
- have known you well for at least two years, such as a friend or colleague

Some people can't be a certificate provider. See the list in the Guide, part A10.

Witnesses

You can't witness your attorneys' signatures and they can't witness yours. Anyone else over 18 years old can be a witness.

People you might want to include in your LPA

Replacement attorneys

You don't have to appoint replacement attorneys but they help protect your LPA. Without them, your LPA might not work if one of your original attorneys stops acting for you.

People to notify

'People to notify' add security. They can raise concerns about your LPA before it's registered – for example, if they think you are under pressure to make the LPA.

LP1H Health and welfare (03.17)

227

Office of the
Public Guardian

Lasting power of attorney for health and welfare

Section 1
The donor

You are appointing other people to make decisions on your behalf.
You are 'the donor'.

Restrictions – you must be at least 18 years old and be able to understand and make decisions for yourself (called 'mental capacity').

Title   First names

Last name

Any other names you're known by (optional – eg your married name)

Date of birth

Day   Month   Year

Address

Postcode

Email address (optional)

For OPG office use only

LPA registration date   OPG reference number

Day   Month   Year

Only valid with the official stamp here.

Help?

For help with this section, see the Guide, part A1.

If you are filling this in for a friend or relative and they can no longer make decisions independently, they can't make an LPA. See the Guide 'Before you start' for more information.

LP1H Health and welfare (07.15)

1

228

Section 2
The attorneys

The people you choose to make decisions for you are called your 'attorneys'. Your attorneys don't need special legal knowledge or training. They should be people you trust and know well. Common choices include your husband, wife or partner, son or daughter, or your best friend.

You need at least one attorney, but you can have more.

You'll also be able to choose 'replacement attorneys' in section 4. They can step in if one of the attorneys you appoint here can no longer act for you.

Restrictions – Attorneys must be at least 18 years old and must have mental capacity to make decisions.

Help?

For help with this section, see the Guide, part A2.

Title	First names		Title	First names

Last name

Last name

Date of birth

Day   Month   Year

Date of birth

Day   Month   Year

Address

Postcode

Address

Postcode

Email address (optional)

Email address (optional)

229

Title	First names

Last name

Date of birth

Day   Month   Year

Address

Postcode

Email address (optional)

Title	First names

Last name

Date of birth

Day   Month   Year

Address

Postcode

Email address (optional)

More attorneys – I want to appoint more than 4 attorneys. Use Continuation sheet 1.

230

Section 3
How should your attorneys make decisions?

You need to choose whether your attorneys can make decisions on their own or must agree some or all decisions unanimously.

Whatever you choose, they must always act in your best interests.

☐ **I only appointed one attorney** (turn to section 4)

How do you want your attorneys to work together? (tick one only)

☐ **Jointly and severally**

Attorneys can make decisions on their own or together. Most people choose this option because it's the most practical. Attorneys can get together to make important decisions if they wish, but can make simple or urgent decisions on their own. It's up to the attorneys to choose when they act together or alone. It also means that if one of the attorneys dies or can no longer act, your LPA will still work.

If one attorney makes a decision, it has the same effect as if all the attorneys made that decision.

☐ **Jointly**

Attorneys must agree unanimously on every decision, however big or small. Remember, some simple decisions could be delayed because it takes time to get the attorneys together. If your attorneys can't agree a decision, then they can only make that decision by going to court.

Be careful – if one attorney dies or can no longer act, all your attorneys become unable to act. This is because the law says a group appointed 'jointly' is a single unit. Your LPA will stop working unless you appoint at least one replacement attorney (in section 4).

☐ **Jointly for some decisions, jointly and severally for other decisions**

Attorneys must agree unanimously on some decisions, but can make others on their own. If you choose this option, you must list the decisions your attorneys should make jointly and agree unanimously on Continuation sheet 2. The wording you use is important. There are examples in the Guide, part A3.

Be careful – if one of your attorneys dies or can no longer act, none of your attorneys will be able to make any of the decisions you've said should be made jointly. Your LPA will stop working for those decisions unless you appoint at least one replacement attorney (in section 4). Your original attorneys will still be able to make any of the other decisions alongside your replacement attorneys.

Help?

For help with this section, see the Guide, part A3.

If you choose 'jointly for some decisions...', you may want to take legal advice, particularly if the examples in part A3 of the Guide don't match your needs.

231

Section 4
Replacement attorneys

This section is optional, but we recommend you consider it

Replacement attorneys are a backup in case one of your original attorneys can't make decisions for you any more.

Reasons replacement attorneys step in – if one of your original attorneys dies, loses capacity, no longer wants to be your attorney or is no longer legally your husband, wife or civil partner.

Restrictions – replacement attorneys must be at least 18 years old and have mental capacity to make decisions.

Help?

For help with this section, see the Guide, part A4.

Title	First names		Title	First names

Last name		Last name

Date of birth			Date of birth		
Day	Month	Year	Day	Month	Year

Address		Address

Postcode		Postcode

☐ **More replacements** – I want to appoint more than two replacements. Use Continuation sheet 1.

When and how your replacement attorneys can act

Replacement attorneys usually step in when one of your **original** attorneys stops acting for you. If there's more than one **replacement** attorney, they will all step in at once. If they **fully** replace your original attorney(s) at once, they will usually act jointly. You can change some aspects of this, but most people don't. See the Guide, part A4.

You should consider taking legal advice if you want to change how your replacement attorneys act.

☐ I want to change when or how my attorneys can act (optional). Use Continuation sheet 2.

232

Section 5
Life-sustaining treatment

 This is an important part of your LPA.

You must choose whether your attorneys can give or refuse consent to life-sustaining treatment on your behalf.

Life-sustaining treatment means care, surgery, medicine or other help from doctors that's needed to keep you alive, for example:
• a serious operation, such as a heart bypass or organ transplant
• cancer treatment
• artificial nutrition or hydration (food or water given other than by mouth)

Whether some treatments are life-sustaining depends on the situation. If you had pneumonia, a simple course of antibiotics could be life-sustaining.

Decisions about life-sustaining treatment can be needed in unexpected circumstances, such as a routine operation that didn't go as planned.

You can use section 7 of this LPA to let your attorneys know more about your preferences in particular circumstances (this is optional).

Help?

For help with this section, including how your LPA relates to an 'advance decision', see the Guide, part A5.

Who do you want to make decisions about life-sustaining treatment? (sign only one option)

Option A – I give my attorneys authority	Option B – I do not give my attorneys authority
to give or refuse consent to life-sustaining treatment on my behalf.	to give or refuse consent to life-sustaining treatment on my behalf.
If you choose this option, your attorneys can speak to doctors on your behalf as if they were you.	If you choose this option, your doctors will take into account the views of the attorneys and of people who are interested in your welfare as well as any written statement you may have made, where it is practical and appropriate.

Signature or mark

Signature or mark

Date signed or marked

Day   Month   Year

Date signed or marked

Day   Month   Year

Witness

The witness must not be an attorney or replacement attorney appointed under this LPA, and must be aged 18 or over.

Signature or mark

Full name of witness

Address

Postcode

Only valid with the official stamp here.

LP1H Health and welfare (07.15)

6

233

Section 6
People to notify when the LPA is registered

This section is optional

You can let people know that you're going to register your LPA. They can raise any concerns they have about the LPA – for example, if there was any pressure or fraud in making it.

When the LPA is registered, the person applying to register (you or one of your attorneys) must send a notice to each 'person to notify'.

You can't put your attorneys or replacement attorneys here.

People to notify can object to the LPA, but only for certain reasons (listed in the notification form LP3). After that, they are no longer involved in the LPA. Choose people who care about your best interests and who would be willing to speak up if they were concerned.

Help?

For help with this section, see the Guide, part A6.

Title   First names

Last name

Address

Postcode

Title   First names

Last name

Address

Postcode

Title   First names

Last name

Address

Postcode

Title   First names

Last name

Address

Postcode

☐ I want to appoint another person to notify (maximum is 5) – use Continuation sheet 1.

Only valid with the official stamp here.

LP1H Health and welfare (07.15)

7

Section 7

Preferences and instructions

This section is optional

You can tell your attorneys how you'd **prefer** them to make decisions, or give them specific **instructions** which they must follow when making decisions.

Most people leave this page blank – you can just talk to your attorneys so they understand how you want them to make decisions for you.

Preferences

Your attorneys don't have to follow your preferences but they should keep them in mind. For examples of preferences, see the Guide, part A7.

Help?

For help with this section, see the Guide, part A7.

Preferences – use words like 'prefer' and 'would like'

☐ I need more space – use Continuation sheet 2.

Instructions

Your attorneys will have to follow your instructions exactly. For examples of instructions, see the Guide, part A7.

Be careful – if you give instructions that are not legally correct they would have to be removed before your LPA could be registered.

If you want to give instructions, you may want to take legal advice.

Instructions – use words like 'must' and 'have to'

☐ I need more space – use Continuation sheet 2.

Only valid with the official stamp here.

LP1H Health and welfare (07.15)

8

235

 Everyone signing the LPA must read this information

In sections 9 to 11, you, the certificate provider, all your attorneys and your replacement attorneys must sign this lasting power of attorney to form a legal agreement between you (a deed).

By signing this lasting power of attorney, you (the donor) are appointing people (attorneys) to make decisions for you.

LPAs are governed by the Mental Capacity Act 2005 (MCA), regulations made under it and the MCA Code of Practice. Attorneys must have regard to these documents. The Code of Practice is available from www.gov.uk/opg/mca-code or from The Stationery Office.

Your attorneys must follow the principles of the Mental Capacity Act:

1. Your attorneys must assume that you can make your own decisions unless it is established that you cannot do so.
2. Your attorneys must help you to make as many of your own decisions as you can. They must take all practical steps to help you to make a decision. They can only treat you as unable to make a decision if they have not succeeded in helping you make a decision through those steps.
3. Your attorneys must not treat you as unable to make a decision simply because you make an unwise decision.
4. Your attorneys must act and make decisions in your best interests when you are unable to make a decision.
5. Before your attorneys make a decision or act for you, they must consider whether they can make the decision or act in a way that is less restrictive of your rights and freedom but still achieves the purpose.

Your attorneys must always act in your best interests. This is explained in the Application guide, part A8, and defined in the MCA Code of Practice.

Before this LPA can be used it must be registered by the Office of the Public Guardian (OPG). Your attorneys can only use this LPA if you don't have mental capacity.

Cancelling your LPA: You can cancel this LPA at any time, as long as you have mental capacity to do so. It doesn't matter if the LPA has been registered or not. For more information, see the Guide, part D.

Your will and your LPA: Your attorneys cannot use this LPA to change your will. This LPA will expire when you die. Your attorneys must then send the registered LPA, any certified copies and a copy of your death certificate to the Office of the Public Guardian.

Data protection: For information about how OPG uses your personal data, see the Guide, Part D.

Help?

For help with this section, see the Guide, part A8.

Section 9
Signature: donor

By signing on this page I confirm all of the following:

- I have read this lasting power of attorney (LPA) including section 8 'Your legal rights and responsibilities', or I have had it read to me

- I appoint and give my attorneys authority to make decisions about my health and welfare, when I cannot act for myself because I lack mental capacity, subject to the terms of this LPA and to the provisions of the Mental Capacity Act 2005

- I confirm I have chosen either Option A or Option B about life sustaining treatment in section 5 of this LPA

- I have either appointed people to notify (in section 6) or I have chosen not to notify anyone when the LPA is registered

- I agree to the information I've provided being used by the Office of the Public Guardian in carrying out its duties

Be careful

Sign this page and section 5 (and any continuation sheets) before anyone signs sections 10 and 11.

Donor	**Witness**
Signed (or marked) by the person giving this lasting power of attorney and delivered as a deed.	The witness must not be an attorney or replacement attorney appointed under this LPA, and must be aged 18 or over.

Donor

Signed (or marked) by the person giving this lasting power of attorney and delivered as a deed.

Signature or mark

Date signed or marked

Day   Month   Year

You must also sign Section 5 (page 6) at the same time as you sign this page.

If you have used Continuation sheets 1 or 2 you must sign and date each continuation sheet at the same time as you sign this page.

If you can't sign this LPA you can make a mark instead. If you can't sign or make a mark you can instruct someone else to sign for you, using Continuation sheet 3.

Witness

The witness must not be an attorney or replacement attorney appointed under this LPA, and must be aged 18 or over.

Signature or mark

Full name of witness

Address

Postcode

Help? For help with this section, see the Guide, part A9.

Section 10
Signature: certificate provider

 Only sign this section after the donor has signed section 9

The 'certificate provider' signs to confirm they've discussed the lasting power of attorney (LPA) with the donor, that the donor understands what they're doing and that nobody is forcing them to do it. The 'certificate provider' should be either:

- someone who has known the donor personally for at least 2 years, such as a friend, neighbour, colleague or former colleague
- someone with relevant professional skills, such as the donor's GP, a healthcare professional or a solicitor

A certificate provider **can't** be one of the attorneys.

Help?

For help with this section, see the Guide, part A10.

Certificate provider's statement

I certify that, as far as I'm aware, at the time of signing section 9:

- the donor understood the purpose of this LPA and the scope of the authority conferred under it
- no fraud or undue pressure is being used to induce the donor to create this LPA
- there is nothing else which would prevent this LPA from being created by the completion of this instrument

By signing this section I confirm that:

- I am aged 18 or over
- I have read this LPA, including section 8 'Your legal rights and responsibilities'
- there is no restriction on my acting as a certificate provider
- the donor has chosen me as someone who has known them personally for at least 2 years **OR**
- the donor has chosen me as a person with relevant professional skills and expertise

Restrictions – the certificate provider must not be:
- an attorney or replacement attorney named in this LPA or any other LPA or enduring power of attorney for the donor
- a member of the donor's family or of one of the attorneys' families, including husbands, wives, civil partners, in-laws and step-relatives
- an unmarried partner, boyfriend or girlfriend of either the donor or one of the attorneys (whether or not they live at the same address)
- the donor's or an attorney's business partner
- the donor's or an attorney's employee
- an owner, manager, director or employee of a care home where the donor lives

Certificate provider

Title   First names

Last name

Address

Postcode

Signature or mark

Date signed or marked

Day   Month   Year

Only valid with the official stamp here.

LP1H Health and welfare (07.15)

11

Section 11

Signature: attorney or replacement

 Only sign this section after the certificate provider has signed section 10

All the attorneys and replacement attorneys need to sign.
There are 4 copies of this page – make more copies if you need to.

By signing this section I understand and confirm all of the following:

- I am aged 18 or over

- I have read this lasting power of attorney (LPA) including section 8 'Your legal rights and responsibilities', or I have had it read to me

- I have a duty to act based on the principles of the Mental Capacity Act 2005 and to have regard to the Mental Capacity Act Code of Practice

- I must make decisions and act in the best interests of the donor

- I must take into account any instructions or preferences set out in this LPA

- I can make decisions and act only when this LPA has been registered

- I can make decisions and act only when the donor lacks mental capacity

Help?

For help with this section, see the Guide, part A11.

Further statement by a replacement attorney: I understand that I have the authority to act under this LPA only after an original attorney's appointment is terminated. I must notify the Public Guardian if this happens.

Attorney or replacement attorney	**Witness**
Signed (or marked) by the attorney or replacement attorney and delivered as a deed.	The witness must not be the donor of this LPA, and must be aged 18 or over.

Signature or mark

Signature or mark

Date signed or marked

Day Month Year

Full names of witness

Title First names

Address

Last name

Postcode

239

Section 11

Signature: attorney or replacement

 Only sign this section after the certificate provider has signed section 10

All the attorneys and replacement attorneys need to sign.
There are 4 copies of this page – make more copies if you need to.

By signing this section I understand and confirm all of the following:

• I am aged 18 or over

• I have read this lasting power of attorney (LPA) including section 8 'Your legal rights and responsibilities', or I have had it read to me

• I have a duty to act based on the principles of the Mental Capacity Act 2005 and to have regard to the Mental Capacity Act Code of Practice

• I must make decisions and act in the best interests of the donor

• I must take into account any instructions or preferences set out in this LPA

• I can make decisions and act only when this LPA has been registered

• I can make decisions and act only when the donor lacks mental capacity.

Further statement by a replacement attorney: I understand that I have the authority to act under this LPA only after an original attorney's appointment is terminated. I must notify the Public Guardian if this happens.

Help?

For help with this section, see the Guide, part A11.

Attorney or replacement attorney	**Witness**
Signed (or marked) by the attorney or replacement attorney and delivered as a deed.	The witness must not be the donor of this LPA, and must be aged 18 or over.

Signature or mark	Signature or mark

Date signed or marked

Day   Month   Year

Full names of witness

Title   First names

Address

Last name

Postcode

240

Section 11

Signature: attorney or replacement

 Only sign this section after the certificate provider has signed section 10

All the attorneys and replacement attorneys need to sign.
There are 4 copies of this page – make more copies if you need to.

By signing this section I understand and confirm all of the following:

- I am aged 18 or over
- I have read this lasting power of attorney (LPA) including section 8 'Your legal rights and responsibilities', or I have had it read to me
- I have a duty to act based on the principles of the Mental Capacity Act 2005 and to have regard to the Mental Capacity Act Code of Practice
- I must make decisions and act in the best interests of the donor
- I must take into account any instructions or preferences set out in this LPA
- I can make decisions and act only when this LPA has been registered
- I can make decisions and act only when the donor lacks mental capacity

Help?

For help with this section, see the Guide, part A11.

Further statement by a replacement attorney: I understand that I have the authority to act under this LPA only after an original attorney's appointment is terminated. I must notify the Public Guardian if this happens.

Attorney or replacement attorney

Signed (or marked) by the attorney or replacement attorney and delivered as a deed.

Signature or mark

Date signed or marked

Day   Month   Year

Title   First names

Last name

Witness

The witness must not be the donor of this LPA, and must be aged 18 or over.

Signature or mark

Full names of witness

Address

Postcode

Section 11
Signature: attorney or replacement

 Only sign this section after the certificate provider has signed section 10

All the attorneys and replacement attorneys need to sign.
There are 4 copies of this page – make more copies if you need to.

By signing this section I understand and confirm all of the following:

- I am aged 18 or over
- I have read this lasting power of attorney (LPA) including section 8 'Your legal rights and responsibilities', or I have had it read to me
- I have a duty to act based on the principles of the Mental Capacity Act 2005 and to have regard to the Mental Capacity Act Code of Practice
- I must make decisions and act in the best interests of the donor
- I must take into account any instructions or preferences set out in this LPA
- I can make decisions and act only when this LPA has been registered
- I can make decisions and act only when the donor lacks mental capacity.

Further statement by a replacement attorney: I understand that I have the authority to act under this LPA only after an original attorney's appointment is terminated. I must notify the Public Guardian if this happens.

Help?

For help with this section, see the Guide, part A11.

Attorney or replacement attorney

Signed (or marked) by the attorney or replacement attorney and delivered as a deed.

Signature or mark

Date signed or marked

Day   Month   Year

Title   First names

Last name

Witness

The witness must not be the donor of this LPA, and must be aged 18 or over.

Signature or mark

Full names of witness

Address

Postcode

Now register your LPA

Before the LPA can be used, it **must** be registered by the Office of the Public Guardian (OPG). Continue filling in this form to register the LPA. See part B of the Guide.

People to notify

If there are any 'people to notify' listed in section 6, you must notify them that you are registering the LPA now. See Part C of the Guide.

Fill in and send each of them a copy of the form to notify people – LP3.

When you sign section 15 of this form, you are confirming that you've sent forms to the 'people to notify'.

Register now

You do not have to register immediately, but it's a good idea in case you've made any mistakes. If you delay until after the donor loses mental capacity, it will be impossible to fix any errors. This could make the whole LPA invalid and it will not be possible to register or use it.

243

Register your lasting power of attorney

Section 12
The applicant

You can only apply to register if you are the donor or attorney(s) for this LPA. The donor and attorney(s) should not apply together.

Who is applying to register the LPA? (tick one only)

☐ **Donor** – the donor needs to sign section 15

☐ **Attorney(s)** – If the attorneys were appointed jointly (in section 3) then they **all** need to sign in section 15. Otherwise, only one of the attorneys needs to sign

Help?

For help with this section, see the Guide, part B2.

Write the name and date of birth for each attorney that is applying to register the LPA. Don't include any attorneys who are not applying.

Title   First names

Last name

Date of birth

Day   Month   Year

Title   First names

Last name

Date of birth

Day   Month   Year

Title   First names

Last name

Date of birth

Day   Month   Year

Title   First names

Last name

Date of birth

Day   Month   Year

244

Section 13
Who do you want to receive the LPA?

We need to know who to send the LPA to once it is registered. We might also need to contact someone with questions about the application.

We already have the addresses of the donor and attorneys, so you don't have to repeat any of those here, unless they have changed.

Who would you like to receive the LPA and any correspondence?

☐ **The donor**

☐ **An attorney** (write name below)

☐ **Other** (write name and address below)

Title   First names

Last name

Company (optional)

Address

Postcode

How would the person above prefer to be contacted?

You can choose more than one.

☐ **Post**

☐ **Phone**

☐ **Email**

☐ **Welsh** (We will write to the person in Welsh)

Help?

For help with this section, see the Guide, part B3.

245

Section 14

Application fee

There's a fee for registering a lasting power of attorney – the amount is shown on the cover sheet of this form or on form LPA120.

The fee changes from time to time. You can check you are paying the correct amount at www.gov.uk/power-of-attorney/how-much-it-costs or call 0300 456 0300. The Office of the Public Guardian can't register your LPA until you have paid the fee.

How would you like to pay?

☐ **Card** For security, **don't** write your credit or debit card details here. We'll contact you to process the payment.

Your phone number

☐ **Cheque** Enclose a cheque with your application.

Help?

For help with this section, see the Guide, part B4.

Reduced application fee

If the donor has a low income, you may not have to pay the full amount. See the Guide, part B4 for details.

☐ **I want to apply to pay a reduced fee**

You'll need to fill in form LPA120 and include it with your application. You'll also **need to send proof** that the donor is eligible to pay a reduced fee.

Are you making a repeat application?

If you've already applied to register an LPA and the Office of the Public Guardian said that it was not possible to register it, you can apply again within 3 months and pay a reduced fee.

☐ **I'm making a repeat application**

Case number

For OPG office use only

Payment reference

Payment date

Day   Month   Year

Amount

246

Section 15
Signature

 Do not sign this section until after sections 9, 10 and 11 have been signed.

The person applying to register the LPA (see section 12) must sign and date this section. This is either the donor or attorney(s) but not both together.

If the **attorneys** are applying to register the LPA and they were appointed to act **jointly** (in section 3), they must all sign.

By signing this section I confirm the following:

- I apply to register the LPA that accompanies this application
- I have informed 'people to notify' named in section 6 of the LPA (if any) of my intention to register the LPA
- I certify that the information in this form is correct to the best of my knowledge and belief

Help?

For help with this section, see the Guide, part B5.

Signature or mark

Signature or mark

Date signed

Day   Month   Year

Date signed

Day   Month   Year

Signature or mark

Signature or mark

Date signed

Day   Month   Year

Date signed

Day   Month   Year

If more than 4 attorneys need to sign, make copies of this page.

247

Check your lasting power of attorney

You don't have to use this checklist, but it'll help you make sure you've completed your LPA correctly.

- [ ] The donor filled in sections 1 to 7.

- [ ] The donor signed both section 5 and section 9 in the presence of a witness. The donor also signed any copies of continuation sheets 1 and 2 that were used, on the same date as signing section 9.

- [ ] The certificate provider signed section 10.

- [ ] All the attorneys and replacement attorneys signed section 11, in the presence of witness(es).

- [ ] Sections 9, 10 and 11 were signed in order. Section 9 must have been signed first, then section 10, then section 11. They can be dated the same day or different days.

- [ ] The donor or an attorney completed sections 12 to 15. If the attorneys are applying and were appointed 'jointly' (section 3), they have all signed section 15 of this form.

- [ ] I've paid the application fee or applied for a reduced fee. If I've applied for a reduced fee, I've included the required evidence and completed form LPA120A.

- [ ] If there were any people to notify in section 6, I've notified them using form LP3.

- [ ] I've not left out any of the pages of the LPA, even the ones where I didn't write anything or there were no boxes to fill in.

Send to:

**Office of the Public Guardian
PO Box 16185
Birmingham B2 2WH**

APPENDIX VIV
PERSONAL NOTES

[1]https://www.gov.uk/government/publications/domicile-set15/domicile-set15.

[2]shorturl.at/efixS (Explains the nil rate band and residence nil rate band).

[3]shorturl.at/efixS (Explains private residence nil rate band).

[4]https://www.gov.uk/government/publications/inheritance-tax-information-about-small-estates-c5-se-2006.

[5]https://www.pensionsadvisoryservice.org.uk/about-pensions/saving-into-a-pension/pensions-and-tax/the-annual-allowance.

[6]https://listentotaxman.com/uk-tax/tax-guides/guide-death-inheritance-tax-guide-2021.html.

[7]https://www.gov.uk/government/publications/inheritance-tax-main-residence-nil-rate-band-and-the-existing-nil-rate-band.

[8] Trustee Act 1925, section 31 (prevents income vesting at age eighteen).

[9] The Trustee Act 1925, section 31, allows children to become beneficially entitled at the age of eighteen. It needs to be excluded to enable the beneficial age to be brought up beyond eighteen.

[10]https://www.gov.uk/guidance/trusts-and-inheritance-tax (https://www.gov.uk/guidance/trusts-and-inheritance-tax#the-10-year-anniversary-charge).

[11] Inheritance Tax Act 1984 ss 104 and 105, 117, to 121.

[12]https://www.gov.uk/business-relief-inheritance-tax.

[13] Inheritance Tax Act 1984 s115(2) and 116(2).

[14] Inheritance Tax Act 115(3).

[15] Wills Act 1837 as amended by S18A (marriage) and S18C (civil partnership).

[16] https://www.gov.uk/government/publications/inheritance-tax-main-residence-nil-rate-band-and-the-existing-nil-rate-band/inheritance-tax-main-residence-nil-rate-band-and-the-existing-nil-rate-band.

[17] Mental Health Act 1983 and Mental Capacity Act 2005.

[18] Inheritance Tax Act 1984 s89B (1) (c).

[19] https://www.gov.uk/power-of-attorney.

Printed in Great Britain
by Amazon

28031911R20145